BACK TO BILLY

BOOK 1 IN THE BACK TO BILLY SAGA
2ND EDITION

A novel by:
Michael Anthony Giudicissi

Copyright © 2023 by Michael Anthony Giudicissi All Rights Reserved

2nd Edition

No part of this book may be reproduced without written permission from the publisher or author, except for a reviewer who may quote brief passages in a review; nor may any part of this book be reproduced, stored in a retrieval system, or transmitted in any form or by any means electronic, mechanical, photocopying, recording or other, without written permission from the publisher or copyright holders.

This manuscript is a work of fiction. Any names, characters, businesses, places, events, locales, and incidents are either the products of the author's imagination or used in a fictitious manner. Any resemblance to actual persons, living or dead, or actual events is purely coincidental.

Mankind Media, LLC Albuquerque, NM
Email: billythekidridesagain@gmail.com

Editors: Mia Giudicissi and Melanie Hubner
Book Design & Layout: Mary Dolan
Cover Art: Fivrous

9 781088 084724

Retail: $18.50

"Time is a storm in which we are all lost"
William Carlos Williams

AUTHOR'S NOTE

Back to Billy was the first novel that I'd ever written. At the time of its publication in 2020, it was considered a complete work. If you've followed the series, you'll know that the story has run on for 5 additional books, with several more planned or on the way. While subsequent books got better (from this writer's perspective), and became easier to write, I always had an apprehension about my story telling in this first book in the series.

As I prepped this Back to Billy series for wider distribution, I decided that among all of the books, this one would get a complete rewrite. My skills as a writer were limited the first time around, and as the entry point to the strange tale of Martin Teebs, Billy the Kid, and Rosita Luna, I felt I owed it to my readers to bring this book up to the standards of the others.

The book you are reading now has some ten thousand additional words versus the first edition. I used those words to clarify and explain some of the key scenes in the book, but not to dramatically change any. Going through this process, it was remarkable to me that so few things actually needed changing in order to fit with the rest of the series.

This is it, there will be no more changes to the opening salvo of my Back to Billy series. If you've read the first edition, I think you'll enjoy this improved version. If this is your first exposure to the series, I'd leave the first edition alone and enjoy this one. There's more to come from the gang in Lincoln, NM and this is your ticket to take the journey with them!

Thanks,

Michael Anthony Giudicissi
December 2022

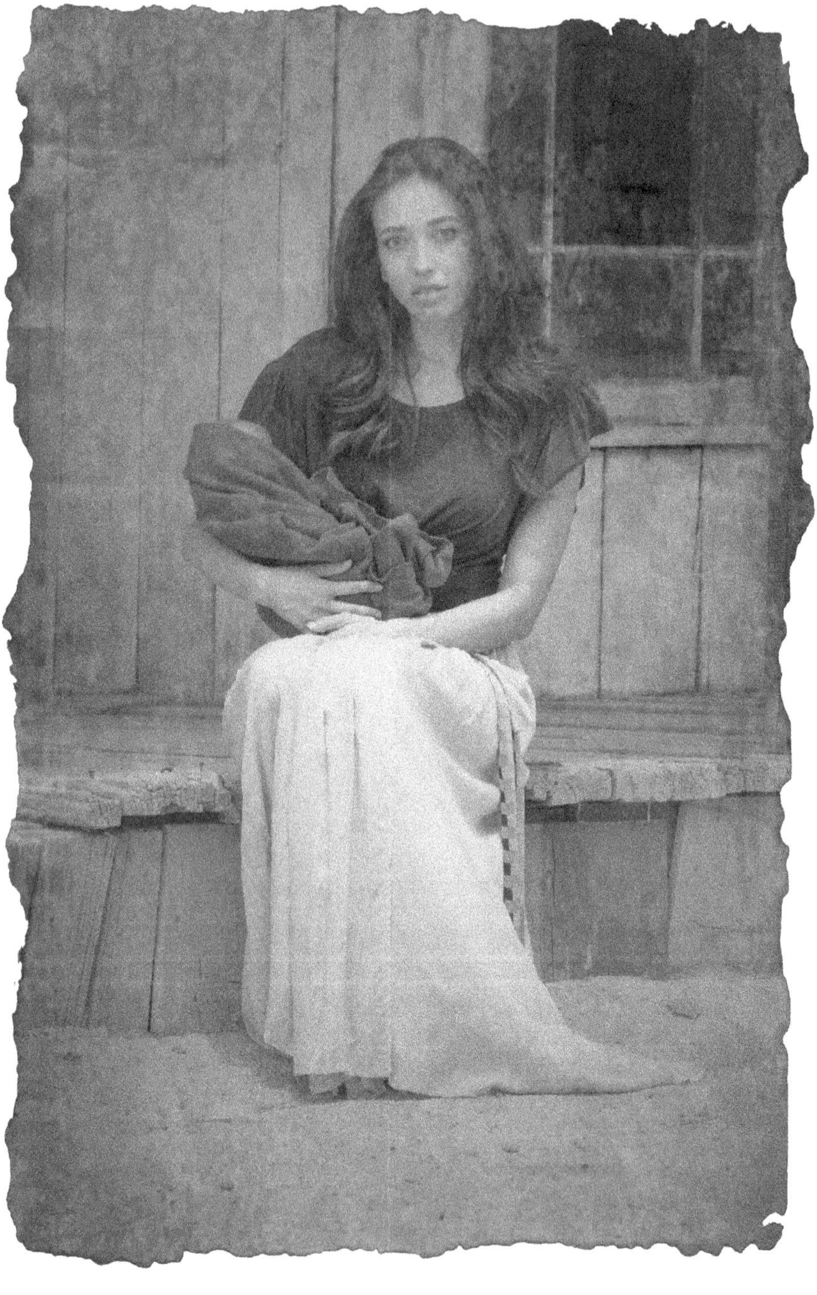

1.

Lincoln, NM November 1878

The big man hit the ground hard in the center of Lincoln's main (and only) street with a puff of dust escaping his clothes into the air. And then in a fashion very similar to the way he arrived in town, he was gone. Disappeared. Vanished into thin air almost as he'd never even existed.

"Teebs! What the hell?" yelled "Big Jim" French, confused, and then turning to Billy, "Where in the hell did he go Kid?"

French was at least 10 years older, although in those times no one paid particular attention to your birth certificate, if you even had one. One might believe with his extra decade of life experience, he might know better than to ask a question that clearly had no answer. Billy, for his part, just stared sadly at the blank spot that used to contain his friend. It's not as if this was the first time Billy saw Martin Teebs up and vanish (or up and appear from thin air) but this time felt more permanent, as if he just lost his best friend without even a chance to say goodbye.

Billy and French stared for just a moment more into the void as a lonely dust devil spun up and flitted away, but the approach of a couple of deputies along with a posse snapped them immediately back to reality. Billy had just shot and killed his two guards while escaping from "The House", Lincoln's largest building and home of the Murphy/Dolan empire, where he'd been held prisoner for over a week.

"Let's git the hell out of here Frenchie. Time to say goodbye to Lincoln for a spell!" proclaimed Billy slapping French hard on his shoulder. Surveying the quickly approaching mass of guns, balls, and bloodlust French nodded in assent as his feet revved up and built up a head of steam. Neither of the men could run faster than the posse's bullets, but at minimum they needed to get behind some cover before they were the ones hitting the dirt on main street with a thud. They ran off Lincoln's only street, once called the most dangerous street in America, with guns still drawn. They quickly made their way into the livery stable where fellow Regulator Jose Chavez y Chavez waited nervously with their mounts. The boys knew Sheriff Peppin's men weren't planning to take prisoners, seeing as Bonney had just single handedly shot his way out of the town's most secure building under the watchful eye of his two best deputies. No, if Billy and company were found, they take a round or ten to the head if they were lucky, and hang in front of the entire town if they weren't.

As Billy took one last turn to where Martin vanished, a great wailing cry was heard as the news of his disappearance spread throughout Lincoln. The most beautiful woman in the territory, Rosita Luna, known as The Belle of Lincoln had just learned that her beau Martin was gone, missing, disappeared with no prospect of return. She sprinted to the now vacant spot where he last existed, screaming his name again and again, dropping to her knees on the spot he last manned, pounding her fists to the ground. "*Martin! Martin!* Come back!" the poor woman wailed, trying to force her words through the very fabric of time.

Billy sighed as he ran, wishing he could help the young woman, but knowing that he'd be no help to her, his friend Martin, or anyone else if he was dead, and dead was a very distinct possibility at the moment if he didn't get out of Lincoln. "Teebsie," Billy whispered to himself, "you sure picked a hell of a time to leave."

2.

Manchester, NH 1975

"Faster Arlo!" screamed a very pregnant Sheila Teebs, looking across the front seat to her husband. With their first child firmly in the clutches of labor, and making a strong play to get out into the world *right now*, their old psychedelic Econoline van screamed down the Everett Turnpike in search of the Catholic Medical Center emergency room. "Like, chill babe, I'm going as fast as I can!" replied Arlo, "You don't wanna, like, get into an accident before we even get there do you?".

Sheila bit her lip both in the throes of a powerful contraction and to keep from saying something that Arlo would surely regret. A flushed, angry look crossed her face, but screaming at the man who took part in making this new life would hardly help her feel any better. Finally, as the gripping contraction passed, she said, "Well, I don't want to have this baby here in your dirty old van!"

Arlo couldn't help but laugh out loud at the joke that was already forming in his head. If not for the fat joint he'd smoked an hour before, he might have had enough self-control to keep it to himself. Pot always lowered his inhibitions, which is probably why he liked it so much, and smoked it so often. "Why not babe?" he teased, "We made him in this van…remember? We might as well have him here too!". Arlo howled in delight at the joke as Sheila slipped into the throes of another powerful contraction. Saying nothing, she reached down to her belly and just glared at the man she'd only decided to marry a year before.

Sheila and Arlo had met at Woodstock where they both indeed did eat the brown acid. They hit it off almost immediately, both having lost their group of friends by the end of day one of the concert. A student at Saint Anselm college, Sheila was a bright intellectual with a strong bent for fashion. Arlo on the other hand, barely escaped high school with a diploma and had been working odd jobs ever since graduation. He was the fun, carefree kind of guy that Sheila rarely met at school and she found him charmingly goofy. Arlo smoked a lot of pot, loved to listen to music and railed stridently against Nixon the Vietnam War. The unlikely pair consummated their two day relationship near the vats of granola at Woodstock and had been together ever since.

With the soon to be arrival of baby Teebs, Arlo had landed a job as an intern at an advertising agency. Had he been dropped onto the surface of the moon, he'd have been in a more fitting environment than a professional office such as he was from 9am to 5pm each day. He wore a shirt and tie every day, a look that he took to calling a monkey suit and likened to being in prison. Labeling nearly everyone he worked with as "squares", Arlo nevertheless decided that it was time for him to be the responsible one so that Sheila could stay home with the baby. They had rented a small two-bedroom home in nearby Hooksett and got started on the serious business of living like real adults. Arlo had promised Sheila that he was a good bet, and despite his complaining about the job, he seemed to be paying off.

"FASTER!" screamed Sheila as she was sure the baby's head must be poking its way out of the birth canal based on the very sudden increase in pain. Arlo went heavy on the gas pedal and stormed off their exit quickly, gliding into the ER entrance and artfully to a stop in front of the glass doors. He ran around the side of the van and yanked Sheila's door open.

"Hey, like my wife's having a baby!" Arlo yelled to no one in particular as they shuffled in through the double doors. A very professional looking nurse walked quickly toward them taking Sheila's arm. "Ok, I've got her" said the nurse calmly, "Is this your first honey?". Relieved at not having to tell her baby that it had been born in a Budweiser box in the back of its father's van, Sheila pushed her words out through labored breaths, "Yes, it's my…I mean our first". The nurse glanced over at Arlo who put both thumbs into the air, as if some sort of reward or compliment to the woman for a job well done.

"What's your name darling?" asked the nurse as she shuttled Sheila toward another set of double doors, leading deeper in the bowels of the hospital

"It's Sheila, Sheila Teebs" she answered as baby Teebs made his imminent presence known one more time. Sheila howled in pain as Arlo looked helplessly and nervously on.

"You say here," said the nurse as kindly as you can when you're giving someone orders, "I'll let you know when the baby arrives." The nurse motioned towards a bank of chairs and firmly pointed Arlo to choose one. Being that he wasn't given any other option, he dumbly nodded his head and blew a kiss to his wife.

"C'mon Sheila, let's go have a baby!" said the nurse as the double doors swung closed leaving Arlo sitting in the lobby, staring in fear and wonderment at what was about to happen, and how it would change their lives, and their baby's…forever.

3.

Arlo wheeled Sheila slowly down the hall to the nursery so she could get another look at their new bouncing baby boy. The delivery was excruciating and lasted for hours. At least three times, Arlo had to let the charge nurse know that he was stepping out to his van. Once there, he'd roll another fat joint, smoke it, and be calm enough to slip back inside and torture his ass for a few more hours on the rock hard chairs.

"10 pounds! You did it babe, you made a BIG old baby Teebs!" said Arlo proudly, looking down upon his son who was clearly the biggest baby behind the giant glass panel.

Cries and gurgles were heard from behind the window as Sheila took the first look at her son since they'd cleaned him up and placed him in a powder blue blanket in his bassinette. Swaddled tightly, the boy just laid there, blinking calmly at the new world he'd just been introduced to.

"The fruit of my loins!" proclaimed Arlo then quickly correcting himself, "Uh, well the fruit of *our* loins technically. Sorry babe, didn't mean to leave your loins out of it. I mean, they're good loins. No, great. I love those loins." He smiled warmly at Sheila who looked less the worse for wear than Arlo did at this moment, and she'd not even smoked a single joint. "What should we name him?"

Sheila was thoughtful for a moment and carefully said, "I've been thinking about this. How about naming him after my father. What do you think?" She cast a hopeful glance up at Arlo, trying to determine if he'd be as enthusiastic as she was?

"Herb? Herbert Teebs? Like, that's way too square for a cool little dude like this. Two thumbs down babe. I was thinking of something rad like Buzz, or Scout, or maybe even Sky? Kids these days gotta stand out." added Arlo.

"No son of mine is going to be named Buzz or Scout, thank you" said Sheila firmly and dismissively. Arlo winced a little as he started to come to the realization that he was no longer calling all the shots in his small but growing family.

"I know,"" said Sheila and then after a pause, "How about Martin?" Arlo's eyes aimed towards the ceiling as he mulled the idea and even seemed to mouth the name a time or two without saying it.

"Martin huh? I like it. It's a good strong name. A guy named Martin could do almost anything he wanted to, huh? Ok babe," said Arlo enthusiastically, "From this point forward our little boy shall be known as Martin Teebs!" Arlo thrust his hand joyfully in the air as if making some official proclamation. As he did, he nearly smacked a woman who was walking slowly down the hall with a dark haired gentleman.

"Whoa," offered Arlo, "Like, I didn't even see you there."

"I'm sorry, did you just say Martin? Is that your baby's name?" asked the woman curiously as she peered through the glass at little Martin's bassinette with a smile. Sheila carefully looked them over for a moment, judging them most likely not to be the type to steal a baby from a hospital nursery, especially with the parents standing right there in front of them.

"Why, yes we did. We just decided on his name," said Sheila, surprised, "Why do you ask?"

"Oh it's just that we're here with our grandfather" said the woman, "His name is Martin too. I guess hearing the name just caught me off guard."

The man she was with quickly interjected "Well Grandpa is Martin Jr. to be specific"

"Righteous dude!" barked Arlo, always willing to make a new friend, "What's he in for?"

The man and woman quickly glanced at each other, as if wondering whether to bring down two perfectly happy strangers with the news. The woman spoke first "It's cancer, he's dying. He doesn't have much longer to live". She gave a sad little smile to let Arlo know that it was fine that he asked. Arlo, now wishing he hadn't asked, added "Oh, bummer dude. Sorry."

"It's fine, it's fine, he had a nice long life. He's 94 now" said the man, "He lived down near where they first tested the atomic bomb, during World War II. I guess that's what eventually got him."

Sheila and Arlo looked helplessly at the couple, and even the normally talkative Arlo couldn't think of a single thing to say that would make the situation better. He just stood there, alternately glancing at his son, and shifting side to side on his shoes which made a weird, squeaky sound echoing down the hallway.

After an awkward silence, the man continued "We brought him here for some decent care. He was living in some shit hole in New Mexico. We used to live down that way when we were kids, but luckily we escaped. What was the name of that town again Roni?"

"Lincoln. Lincoln, New Mexico" replied Roni as she noticed the lost look upon the new parent's faces.

"Well, we're so very sorry to hear it," said Sheila finally "We're the Teebs, Arlo and Sheila". Arlo extended his hand as Sheila smiled warmly at Roni.

The man grabbed Arlo's hand while adding "I'm *Tomas*, uh Tom Antrim and this is my sister Ronita. We call her Roni".

As the 4 greeted each other, a light bulb went off in Tom's head and before he could stop it, an idea burst from his lips "You know what might be great? Grandpa loves kids. I'll bet it would really brighten his day if he could meet his little namesake…little Martin. Would you mind bringing him in? Just for a minute or two?"

Arlo looked questioningly down at Sheila as if waiting for her approval. She smiled warmly and nodded her head at Tom, "Sure."

"Alright!" said Arlo, "Let's bust little Martin Teebs outta this joint and let him meet his first new friend!".

A friendly nurse retrieved little ten pound Martin from the nursery and handed him over to Sheila, who cradled the boy gently in her arms. Arlo pushed her down the hall quickly following Tom and Roni into a meeting that no one could have known would fulfill destiny and reverberate through time itself.

4.

Martin Antrim Jr. wasn't really a junior at all. After all, there was no Martin Antrim Sr. He was called Junior as his birth father's name was also Martin, but Junior never knew much more about the man other than that. Born in Lincoln, NM in 1879, Martin Jr. never met his father who had disappeared before his birth, never to return. His mother, Rosita Luna died when Martin was just a toddler. A man named Billy Antrim had known and befriended Junior's father and felt compelled to take young Junior in when news of his mother passed on from this life. Living just outside Lincoln County in Magdalena, NM, Billy and his wife Maria provided a stable loving home for Junior until he reached the age of 17, at which time he determined that he would go back to Lincoln to search for, or wait for, the father he never knew.

Junior would spend his years fruitlessly waiting in the dusty old town hoping against hope that his father, the man his mother adored, would feel compelled to return for his son. Aside from a few fleeting bits of information from Lincoln old timers, Junior never learned much about the mystery man known as Martin Teebs. When work or the occasional visit to Billy and Maria called, Junior would leave Lincoln grudgingly, but always return straight away lest he miss the phantom father that he hoped would someday return. As the years wore on, Junior became more and more bitter. Not only at his father, but at life in general. He married a local girl named Celsa Gomez, who bore him 2 perfectly happy children. Celsa died young, at the age of 28 in the great influenza pandemic of 1918 leaving Junior to care for and raise his children on his own.

Whenever the topic of grandparents came up, Junior deferred his kids to Billy and Maria. His children never needed to know he was in fact a bastard, cast aside by a worthless prick that didn't have the decency to marry his mother or have the slightest interest in meeting his son, or so Junior had convinced himself.

As his children grew up and had children of their own, Junior settled deeper and deeper into Lincoln, now a bustling "old west" attraction because of its association with William H. Bonney better known as Billy the Kid. It was as if Junior had grown roots deep into the valley's soil and no one, or no thing could pull him away. If Junior were to ponder whether he actually *liked* living in the small town, he'd be given cause to pause before answering. More than liking it, he felt compelled to stay there by the vacant memory a missing man who stubbornly refused to be found or to return.

In Lincoln, nothing changed. It was as if the town had come to a grinding halt when the McSween house burned to the ground during the 5 Day Battle, and never got its engine started again. Tourists loved the appeal of the trapped-in-time little village that sheltered not only The Kid, but the Regulators, Jesse Evans, Pat Garrett, and other old west luminaries. Junior, on the other hand, hated it. It was a constant reminder of what he'd lost as a young child, and seemingly would never have again. If Junior ever suspected that his adopted father Billy Antrim was actually Billy the Kid, he never let on for fear of divulging a secret that could impact them all. There were many coincidences and at one point Junior decided that either Billy must have been the Kid, or perhaps even his father Martin Teebs was the infamous outlaw? Could that be the reason he failed to return to the old county seat? Was Martin Teebs afraid that returning to the scene of his crimes, even decades later, would entice a death sentence that his son would be forced to see administered? Try as he might, Junior simply couldn't believe he was the son of Billy the Kid, and everyone knew that Pat Garret had shot and killed The Kid back in 1881 in Fort Sumner anyway.

Approaching 90 years old in 1969, Junior had incredibly lived from the closing salvos of the Lincoln County War all the way to see American ensconced in the Vietnam War. His health was failing but despite urgings from his few friends, he resisted traveling to El Paso or Albuquerque to seek better medical care than was available locally. Dr. Julie Riley was a fine physician, the great granddaughter of Dr. Jules Riley who founded a clinic in the town at the turn of the century, but there was a limit to what she could do with the stubborn patient. Finally in 1973 Junior was rushed to Roswell for diagnosis after coughing up blood for several days at a time. The diagnosis was grim, lung cancer. The prognosis was worse, 6 months or less to live.

Never one to spend much time away from his home, lest he miss a desperate attempt by his father to reach him, Junior willed himself well enough to leave the hospital and made his way back to his tiny home in Lincoln. 6 months came and went and Junior stubbornly held onto life, almost as he was going to spite it by continuing to live. At times, the coughing fits were so intense he would pass out, falling to the old wooden floor. Once, his sleeve briefly caught on fire as he fell into the fireplace. Luckily the intense pain quickly brought him back to reality and he was able to extinguish it with minimal damage.

In the Fall of 1974 Junior was visited by his 2 grandchildren Tomas and Ronita. They had received letters from neighbors imploring them to come and care for their grandfather. While Junior was delighted to see them, he firmly resisted any hint that he might ever leave Lincoln alive. While certainly a fool's errand to believe that his long lost father, who would now be over 130 years old if he somehow managed to cheat time, would still come back for him, Junior vowed to meet the man in Lincoln, or in Hell. Day after day he stared out of his front door, only adorned by an ancient rusty dented metal bucket that his mother for some reason had treasured. While he couldn't remember, he was later told by his grandmother Lourdes that the bucket was but the last thing Junior's mother had to remember the man she desperately loved. Junior kept it more because of his mother's connection to it, rather than his father's. Closing in on the grave, Junior figured that if he ever met the man who sired him, he could strap the bucket across the man's face to catch all of the bullshit that would surely be coming from his mouth, lie after lie about how and why he'd abandoned his own family.

By early 1975 Junior had become so ill that a traveling physician called his grandkids and told them that their grandfather probably wouldn't last a week and they should make arrangements for his soon to be demise and burial. Tomas and Ronita quickly returned to Lincoln and this time, convinced (or demanded) the severely infirmed Junior that he would be coming with them back to New Hampshire.

Arriving at Catholic Medical Center in July of 1975, Junior was quickly moved into the hospice ward and given palliative care and medication for his pain. Near death, he spent most of his days heavily medicated and asleep. It was just a matter of time.

Tomas and Ronita took shifts staying with him until Friday July 4th. On that day they both decided to spend the day, or the weekend if need be to see their crusty but beloved grandfather off to the afterlife. It was the least they could do to honor the man with whom they'd had so many wonderful childhood memories.

With Junior sleeping they walked through the hallways to the cafeteria and came across a young couple who had just had their first child. The father of that child wildly waved his arms around while speaking to the mother. Nearly poking Ronita's eye out the new father and mother quickly apologized, excited as they were that their new baby had finally joined them after 9 months in utero. That child's name….was Martin Teebs

5.

"Grandpa look! We have a surprise for you". Ronita's excited words stirred the old man momentarily from his drug induced stupor.

"Yeah Pa, this little guy was just born and has the same name as you. Meet little Martin" Tomas added.

Junior slid himself slightly up on the bed to get a better look at his new namesake. A thin young man and a woman in a wheelchair tentatively made their way into the room. The woman was holding a baby that dwarfed most newborns that Junior had ever seen. For some reason though, the baby's innocence gave him some peace and for a moment he felt better, almost alive again.

Arlo wheeled Sheila closer to the bed and she asked, "Would you like to hold him?" with a warm smile on her face. Junior was barely able to croak out an answer but managed a half smiling, half grimacing "Ok".

Sheila gently laid little Martin in old Martin's hands as Arlo smiled. Feeling that somehow they had done a good deed, the Teebs turned back to Tom and Roni to talk more about whatever adults talk about in the room and presence of a dying man. Junior gently touched the baby's head which elicited a smile from young Martin and a gurgle which in some circles could have been a laugh, or perhaps the beginning of a cry. The physical contact brought back a flood of memories of his own children, born and raised in Lincoln so many years ago. Junior's failing eyes misted over just a bit. Where had his life gone? In one moment he was a boy chasing snakes and scorpions in the desert outside of Magdalena, and the next he was a virtual prisoner in a hospice ward in a hospital so far from his home he might as well have been on the moon. He'd spent his entire life waiting for, and dreaming about the man that had created him, or had Junior actually wasted his life on that pursuit? Now, dying, he laid in his stale hospital bed knowing the end was near and his dream would never be fulfilled.

"So, Arlo and Sheila Teebs this is your first baby huh? Congratulations!" said Roni. As the name Teebs floated and vibrated against Junior's eardrums he immediately stiffened. The hairs on the back of his neck stood at attention and his entire body went cold. Not cold like he was dying, but cold like he was enraged. The final pieces of his broken life assembled and fell into place as if on command. Without a doubt, and within a nanosecond he realized the baby he was holding was his own father, Martin Teebs Sr.

Unaware of the drama developing on the hospital bed just a few feet away, Arlo proudly responded "Yeah, but he's just the first of many, right babe?" giving Sheila a playful pinch "We're gonna create our own little Teebs dynasty!"

Junior's eyes opened wide with anger. Staring at the baby's innocent face he finally spoke in a low, threatening tone, "You? You little son of a bitch. NOW you come back? Here, when my life is over? You worthless prick!"

With the 4 adults locked in their own conversation, Junior continued "I waited my whole damn life for you to come back, and this is what I get?" Finally Junior could contain himself no more, screaming "Screw you, asshole!!" at little Martin.

Startled by the sudden commotion, the adults turned while Roni rushed to the bedside. "Papa! What in God's name are you doing?" she demanded.

Not nearly done unloading his barrels at the baby, Junior quickly composed himself and pasted on a confused little smile. "Uh, oh nothing. I'm sorry, I just had a shooting pain in my, my uh, backside. I'm ok now." As if to show he was truly fine, Junior lifted little Martin close to his cheek and put on a huge fake smile, saying "We're fine now, we're fine." Arlo looked over to Sheila to make sure they shouldn't make a run for it. Sheila's eyes darted from the dying man back to her husband. Satisfied that it had all been a misunderstanding, she quietly nodded to her husband.

Placated for the moment, the 4 adults turned back to their conversation while Junior scanned his faded memory for any last (or first) words he had planned for the moment he'd meet his father. In a threatening whisper, he continued "I should kill you myself for what you did to my mother. She loved you, you little bastard. She went to her grave loving you." Junior glanced back to the foursome but his tone clearly wasn't loud enough to alarm them again. "In all those years, you couldn't come back for me? Not even once? Big man, leaving a child to fend for himself. What were you so busy doing? What was so important you had to abandon your family?" Junior waited just a beat, as if the newborn might discover the powers of speech and answer him, but quickly saw the folly of his thinking, "If it weren't for Billy and Maria I wouldn't even be here right now". Junior scanned Martin's face for some sense of remembrance, as if any of this were sinking in to his tiny father's psyche. What he saw however was 1 day old Martin Teebs Sr. purse his lips together, crinkle his eyes and appear to laugh right in the old man's face. Unable to control himself Junior exploded "You think this is funny? You think my life is a joke? You're the damned joke you friggin coward!!"

Stunned, Arlo and Sheila rushed in to grab little Martin from the obviously crazy old man. Arlo got there first, gingerly taking the baby and putting him in Sheila's arms.

"The great Martin Teebs!!" screamed Junior, his voice out of control and dripping with sarcasm.

Unsure of what had just happened, a frantic Roni asked "Oh my God! Is he ok? I'm so sorry!"

With a calm demeanor that his boss sometimes hated, Arlo took control of the room "He's fine, yeah." He shot a look at Junior as they prepared to leave, "Dude, chill." Junior's eyes were ablaze with anger, or was it hatred? Tomas and Roni desperately tried to comfort the old man who was still in the throes of whatever had agitated him and offered to Arlo and Sheila as they quickly wheeled out of the room "It's all the medication he's on. He just can't control himself."

Arlo pushed Sheila out of the door with a backward wave of his hand and Junior took his parting shot, screaming to be heard over the din of his now blaring monitors, "Read any good books lately, you little shit??!!"

And with that, Martin Antrim Teebs Junior's unhappy life came to an abrupt end. With rapidly increasing frequency his EKG monitor warned of impending doom as his eyes went wide and a maniacal smile spread across his face. With one long beep his heart stopped and his body went limp, finally having talked to the father he'd spent a lifetime waiting for. The flatlined drone of the monitor followed Arlo, Sheila, and Martin up the hall and all the way back to the nursery.

6.

At the same moment that little Martin Teebs was being whisked down the hallway of Catholic Health Center, a little boy who would ultimately be named Carl Farber was making a similar appearance hundreds of miles away at Englewood Hospital in New Jersey. While one could easily imagine that little Carl's parents felt as much pride and joy at the new life they brought into the world, the circumstances could barely have been any more different. After resting from a short 3 hour labor, Carl's mother cooed at the boy as a nurse laid him gently on her chest. The nurse looked expectantly around to see where the boy's father might be, as he had not attended the birth and was nowhere to be seen in nearby environs.

"Hilda, Hilda," said the nurse, interrupting the parent-child bonding time, "Where's your husband? Would you like me to find him?"

More than a little embarrassed that her husband had been so missing in action that he'd not yet even met his son, Hilda tried to create some misdirection, "Oh, no…no. Thanks Gertie, he's probably just outside getting some air. I'm sure he'll be up straight away." The nurse smiled with what seemed to be a little sadness as she simply nodded her head, rubbed Carl on the back of his neck, and left the mother and son alone in their room.

Outside, on the hospital grounds, Carl's father lit a cigarette and leaned heavily back against a tree. Now he was a father, he thought to himself. The party, if being married to Hilda could ever be considered a party, was most definitely over. He didn't want the responsible life of a father, but he also didn't want to wear condoms, and so here he was, with an entire other life to be responsible for. While other men bandied about giving out cigars to celebrate their newest family addition, Carl's father simply sneered in disgust at what he'd done. If he could undo it, at this very moment, he most certainly would. If he couldn't he'd have to find some way to live with the notion that his free and easy life was long gone, never to return.

If there were any way to go back in time and change the outcome of this day, Carl's father decided he would have jumped on that train the moment it arrived at the station.

7.

"What in the hell was that all about Arlo?" asked Sheila as they quickly wheeled back toward the nursery. Her eyes were open wide and she swung her head from side to side just to make sure the maniac hadn't been resurrected and was following them back to the nursery.

Still shocked and angered by what he'd just seen it took Arlo a few seconds to respond. "I know, right? It was like that old dude knew little Martin or something. Weird." Arlo made a mental note to remember the old man's name so he might figure out just what in the hell really did happen? While he might be able to hold onto such important information for a day or two, the thick layer of bong residue that was coating his brain was likely to wash it away soon after that.

Sheila held Martin tightly whispering to him "That crazy old coot. You NEVER associate with people like that again. Do you understand baby?" Baby Martin gurgled out a smile and laugh as a nurse lifted him from Sheila's arms and brought him behind the nursery glass.

"Martin Teebs" proudly proclaimed Arlo, pointing at his son, "This kid is going to be a mover, a shaker, hell he might even become President! Martin Teebs is going to light the world on fire!"

8.

Waldwick, NJ 2020

The clock on Martin's computer seemed to be stuck on 4:57 for well more than a minute. Martin surveyed his barren, sterile cubicle, the same one he'd inhabited for the past 17 years. Pencils, he thought. Pencils need sharpening. Martin calculated that he could sharpen 1 pencil per minute and that gravely important task would take him to closing time. As he reached into his drawer he felt a tickle in his nose. Burying his index finger deep into the blackness, Martin pulled out the offender, inspected it, and with some satisfaction flicked it into the trash can. Two extra sharp pencils later the clock finally struck 5pm and paroled Martin from his mundane day. He picked up his briefcase with nothing of importance in it, tossed his jacket over his shoulder and walked down the long hallway to the elevator.

Arriving in the parking garage, his remote chirped while opening the doors of his very sensible sedan, and he was soon on his way to his very sensible home, in a very sensible neighborhood, and his very sensible wife Lilly Teebs.

Martin never aspired to be a middling quality control manager at an ad agency, but much like his father Arlo, he really never aspired to much in the way of work at all. His passions, if you could call them that were fantasy football (although he was never much of an athlete), watching TV, and trying to maintain the greenest, thickest lawn on his block. He occupied the exact same job for 17 years, never seeking a promotion, and certainly never performing like someone who earned one. It's almost as if his work life was frozen like that caveman they found in ice somewhere in the polar north. Martin was exactly what he never wanted to be and he was likely to be that for the rest of his career.

"Lil, I'm home" he announced as he stepped squarely into his middle class living room, and existence. Lilly, if she was anywhere, was probably either doing housework, or reading one of the many books she often read as an escape from her not entirely unpleasant reality.

"Oh, hey Martin. Welcome home hon," said Lilly as she glided into the room from the kitchen. Her oversized tee shirt and yoga pants belied what Martin had always considered a smoking little body on his wife, albeit one he didn't get the pleasure of connecting with very often anymore. Lilly was a cute, petite brunette that Martin had somehow managed to wow while they both attended Rutgers University. Smart and driven in her younger days, Lilly now seemed to have accepted her fate as the wife of a man firmly stuck on "slow" and not having a way out. She dressed as stylishly as their budget would allow, was a wonderful cook, and kept the house in immaculate order.

Martin leaned in and gave his customary peck on the cheek before asking "What's for dinner?"

"I made your favorite" said Lilly, her eyes daring Martin to guess what it was. With no answer forthcoming, she simply replied "Pork chops" to which Martin smiled devilishly. "Oh, and I got your favorite ice cream. Chocolate chip mint. It was on sale, two for 4 dollars" added Lilly.

Martin was a man of value and that his wife could not only prepare his favorite meal on a budget, but also score him 2 half gallons of his favorite dessert pleased him immensely. He strode back to Lilly with purpose, giving her a firm kiss directly on the lips to her shocked surprise. The big man danced down the hallway to change into his old grey sweats and prepare for the feast ahead.

9.

Martin's stomach made the sound that an old engine might, deprived of oil but still having enough gas to fire. He sat bolt upright in bed and checked the clock; 1:30am. "Ohhhh, that was too much ice cream" he moaned to himself. After a visit to the guest room bathroom, he carefully crept down the stairs, and unable to resist the temptation, popped open the freezer and pulled out his minty friend for a rematch.

Martin shuffled into the living room and sat down on the worn but comfortable couch. Unsure of what to do or how much ice cream to eat, he flicked on the TV remote to see what might be showing at this ungodly hour. After passing through several get rich quick, get thin quick, and get fit quick infomercials he stumbled upon the opening credits of a movie he'd never seen before, but was aware of: "Young Guns".

"Never seen this before, how bad could a western with a bunch of kids be?" he mused to himself. Carefully licking the ice cold spoon Martin tried to imagine himself in the old west. He assumed food was scarce and there was no 7-11 on every corner, so he'd likely be thinner than the version of himself that reflected back in the glow of the screen. Envisioning himself as an expert marksman, hunter, lawman, and hero, Martin allowed himself to be absorbed by the movie until he realized it was about a name he'd heard many times but knew relatively nothing about, Billy the Kid.

As the plot unfurled upon screen he found himself entranced by the story of William H. Bonney, wondering how much of what he was seeing was Hollywood's version of The Kid, and how much was real. Martin didn't have to feign ignorance of the subject, he knew literally nothing about Billy or this Lincoln County War. Did The Kid really dance down Main Street brazenly taking the Sheriff's own guns and shooting him dead with them? Did he shoot and kill Henry Hill by shoving the barrel of his gun out of the front of his pants?

"Well, The Kid had balls. I'll give him that" mused Martin as he scooped deeper into the final vestiges of his 2nd dessert.

In the final climatic shootout in Lincoln, The Kid roused his friends for their final stand and Martin couldn't help but root for them. There was poor Charlie Bowdre bemoaning his little Mexican wife that he wanted to get back to. Dirty Steve certainly looked the part covered from head to toe in the flotsam and jetsam of frontier life as he jammed round after round into his rifle. The cultured and refined Doc Scurlock only wished to protect his celestial girlfriend Yen Sun from the despotic Lawrence Murphy and a life of sexual servitude. And finally of course, there was The Kid. Cocky and bold in the face of certain death. Martin was vaguely aware that The Kid died young, hence the name "The Kid" but hoped against hope that he didn't have to watch his demise on screen at that very moment. He'd come to admire the portrayal of Bonney in the movie. Fun, gregarious, loyal, and deadly. These were all of the things that Martin wasn't, well except for the loyal part. He found himself rooting for the underdog fighting against the corruption of Murphy and hoping somehow that all of the Regulators could survive, if for nothing else, so that Martin could watch his new friends in the sequel that he imagined must surely exist?

During the escape from the burning McSween house, The Kid caught several bullets but was able to remain on his mount and ride away. Poor Charlie settled his imaginary feud with John Kinney just before taking one to the chest, while Dirty Steve was cut down when Chavez failed to bring him a horse. Doc and Yen were able to escape as well and live happily, or not, ever after.

Martin breathed a deep sigh of relief when what was left of the Regulators rode out of sight but clenched when Billy rode into view once more. "Get out of there Billy!" he whisper shouted, knowing that Colonel Dudley might again fire up the infamous Gatling Gun and cut The Kid down in his prime.

"Why aren't they shooting at him" he wondered aloud as Billy made a little speech about "reaping it" before shooting Lawrence Murphy dead between the eyes and watching actor Jack Palance give a spectacular fall to his death in the middle of Lincoln's dusty main street.

In the final voiceover Martin learned that Billy continued to ride, never leaving New Mexico and was shot down by the Sheriff Pat Garret in Fort Sumner. Advices say he was unarmed and shot in the dark. A little darkness permeated the already dark room as Martin thought about Billy being ambushed by another legend of the old west that Martin had heard of but knew nothing about.

"Wow, damn." was all Martin could manage as the closing credits rolled. He felt as though he had somehow met a best friend, and then lost him all in the space of two hours. Wide awake now, he checked his watch and saw the time; 3:32am. "Oh man, I'm never going to get any sleep!" he admonished himself and headed to the kitchen to drop the empty ice cream container in the trash, the spoon in the sink, and then padded along the wood floors back to bed.

"Billy the Kid?" he whispered to himself as he lay next to Lilly who was softly snoring, oblivious to Martin's eye-opening experience. Martin replayed the scenes of Billy laughing, smiling, killing, and fighting injustice over and over in his head as he finally drifted off to a fitful sleep.

10.

The next day dawned clear and bright as Martin struggled to wake with the alarm. Lilly just smiled as she popped out of bed and bounded downstairs. Quickly remembering his history lesson from earlier that morning, he made a mental note to check the mall's mega bookstore on the way home to find a book on Billy the Kid and fact check the movie versus the reality of one William H. Bonney. For whatever reason, Martin had been captured by the film. Always the addictive personality, he'd find some obscure thing to be excited about, and then spend all of his time and attention on that thing. While it would probably reap more and better rewards to make Lilly that "thing", Martin was captured by the tale of a young man who lived and died well over a hundred years ago at the moment. Focus locked, he prepared for another 9 hour borefest at work and slipped into the shower.

Later that day, having been paroled from another worthless day at the office, Martin pointed his car toward Paramus, NJ, the land of many shopping malls. Arriving at the bookstore he browsed nonchalantly for a few minutes before realizing he was never going to find what he sought on his own. Breaking down, he asked the clerk for help.

"Umm, excuse me, where would I find history books on the old west?" inquired Martin to the smiling 20 something girl behind the counter.

"Sure sir! If you'll go two aisles down and make a left you'll see our history section. You see where all of those older guys are standing?" she replied.

Indeed, there were a bunch of middle aged men standing in exactly the drop zone that Martin was headed for. Knowing he'd also now be labeled an "older guy" the next time the young lady helped someone, he smiled at her and made his way across the store.

"What the hell are they all doing there" he asked aloud as he made his approach. Instantly Martin realized what must have happened. With the big two-for-one sale on ice cream, he probably wasn't the only middle class schlub that overindulged last night. All of these guys must have awakened to a boiling belly and a date with destiny too. There were 5 men strewn about poring over books about The Kid and the Lincoln County War. One especially overweight guy in a cheap polyester knit short sleeved shirt gave Martin a knowing smile and wink as if to say "welcome to the club". Slightly horrified and embarrassed that he was even here, Martin shoehorned his way between the men and casually, too casually to actually be casual, glanced at the numerous book spines.

"You here to read up on The Kid? Too much fudge ripple last night?" asked Mr. Polyester with way too much gusto.

"Umm, yeah. I just wanted to see what they have. Thanks," said Martin. Impulsively he wanted to leave and not be a part of these, well, what was the word he was searching for…. Losers? Yea, that was it. He was mildly revulsed by the thought that he was just like these fledgling Billy the Kid fans, seeing nothing in common between their shallow, boring lives and his rich, successful one. He decided to press on while Polyester tapped him on the shoulder.

"Here! This one is the best. It's by Sergio Bachaca, 'The True Life Of Billy the Kid'." Mr. Poly shoved book into Martin's hand and the wonderment of it caught him off guard. Here, in 250 pages were all the answers to the questions he didn't even know yet that he'd have. The cover was adorned with a bright painting of The Kid in his infamous crushed hat and crooked smile. He could take this book, right now, go home and become an expert on Billy the Kid (or so he thought). He felt giddy, powerful, and strangely happy at that moment.

"So, this is a good one huh?" asked Martin noncommittally.

"Good? It's the best, most factual account of Billy's life, bar none. I own 3 copies myself," offered Polyester, "I even got one signed by Serge on one of his book tours in Virginia."

The way Polyester said "Serge" bothered Martin. It was as if he knew the man and might text him to have a beer before heading home to his dreadful dead-end life, or so Martin imagined. More than anything Martin wanted himself and his book to be gone from this place. He wanted to be in private so he could read and learn without the balance of these nobodies around to ruin it for him. Just then Martin wondered, did each of the men feel the same way about him?

"Well, thanks. I think I'll take your advice and get this one" offered Martin as he looked to make his exit. One of the men, not smiling, winking, or nodding stood by the edge of the bookcase slowly pulling back book after book with a dismissive look. Martin caught his eye for a second and saw the look of disapproval at his choice of reading material. With sharp features and a permanently dissatisfied look on his face, the stranger sniffed at Martin and turned away, pulling an old flip phone from his corduroy pants as if he might have missed a call. Martin wondered what he could have done to piss off someone he didn't even know?

Making a hasty retreat to the cashier, he paid for his book and looked for his car among the throngs of other sensible sedans in the mall parking lot. Finding it he collapsed into the front seat and removed the book from its bag, tempted to read it right then and there. Martin felt almost an electricity in his fingers as he held the book. It was as if it beckoned him to open and start reading it right now. With the blaring horns, soccer moms talking loudly on their phones, and jumbo jets screaming above on their way to Newark Liberty Airport, Martin knew that this was not the environment he wanted to get to know Billy the Kid in.

"No, not yet" Martin told himself as if not wanting to rush into sex with a woman he just met, "Let's wait until tonight when you and I have more time."

He began to slip the book back into the bag but at the last moment decided to prop it up with Billy facing the windshield. Reaching across the passenger seat, he grabbed and fastened the seatbelt over The Kid to make sure he didn't tumble into the footwell. His little 2 person carpool complete, Martin carefully navigated the swollen parking lot and made his way back home.

11.

Carl Farber stood mutely near the edge of the bookcase in the Paramus Mall's giant bookstore. Unlike the rest of those whom he judged to be losers he hadn't stayed up all night watching 'Young Guns'. Instead, Farber was doing market research. How many middle-aged men would show up to buy Billy the Kid books upon seeing a movie about him on the big or little screen? Farber was interested because he had his own book on The Kid in the works and wanted to understand the economy of it all. While he didn't have a publisher interested, he had a unique viewpoint on his subject that he was sure would generate publishing riches just as soon as he could catch someone's ear. As men came and went in the early evening hours, one in particular caught his eye. A big, fat man in a polyester short sleeved shirt seemed to have something to say to every one of the newly minted Billyphiles who were buzzing about in the history section. He regaled them with his favorite book by Sergio Bachaca and proclaimed it "the best, most accurate history of the life of the boy bandit". More than once under his breath Farber had to hold back a "bullshit" or "fuck off" towards the man so as not to disturb his publishing petri dish.

When a tall man came ambling in, Farber picked up right away that this guy was lost, and a complete novice when it came to Bonney. The man looked even more out of place among the other newbies and was quickly approach by Mr. Polyester who of course, pushed Bachaca's book on him. Farber seethed at the misinformation that was being peddled to this particular group of losers, but relished in the idea that soon, he'd set things straight, once and for all. He imagined someday coming back to this very store to do a dramatic reading of his best-selling book. He smiled to himself at how these clowns would lap up every word of the "new" Billy the Kid….so unlike the pablum they'd been fed by Hollywood. He'd probably need security so he could push his way through the crowd upon signing the very last book. "No more questions, no more questions for Mr. Farber," his bodyguard would say as they hustled him into a waiting Escalade with black tinted windows. Inside, his former Playboy playmate wife would purr erotically, having waited for hours for Farber to arrive and meet her every need. As they clinked their champagne glasses, Farber's dream dissolved into nothing but the bunch of worthless losers in his field of vision. The big man said something to Poly and with what looked like a "thank you" and began to leave. For a moment the two locked eyes and Farber narrowed his face to show his displeasure about the man's choice of books. The big man looked quizzically at him for a moment before pressing by to get to the cashier. Farber watched him until he was out of sight, figuring that he'd have one more easy mark when his sure-to-be bestseller finally hit the shelves later in the year.

As the rest of the men flipped through books that Farber knew were full of lies, he began seeing dollar signs on top of each of their stupid, ignorant heads. Farber smiled a satisfied smile and decided to leave, heading back to his barren one bedroom apartment. If he remembered correctly, he still had one microwave TV dinner left, and with only a little freezer burn to boot.

12.

"Martin! Did you order more stuff from Amazon?" shouted Lilly Teebs on a sunny Saturday morning.

Aroused from his morning routine of drinking a gallon or so of coffee, Martin stirred and walked towards the front door, "Oh, hey! They're here already" he said Martin with a satisfied smile.

"Let me guess, more Billy the Kid books, right?" demanded Lilly, a droll look spreading across her face.

In the two months since purchasing Sergio Bachaca's book at the mall, Martin had become ravenous in his desire to learn everything he could about Billy, The Regulators, and the Lincoln County War. Night after night (and more than a few times, during his numerous slow times at work) he scoured the internet for more books on The Kid, ordering whatever he could find to satisfy his new urge for knowledge. Boxes made regular appearances on the Teebs' neat and tidy porch as Martin stayed up late into the night reading facts, tales, and rumors about a time he only wished he could somehow visit. Wouldn't that be something, he thought to himself, to get to spend just one day back in old Lincoln to see and feel it all for himself? Since time travel was impossible, Martin vowed that he'd learn his way back in time so that he could be as close to his new heroes as possible.

That one night watching Young Guns had somehow changed Martin. Where before he only wanted to make it through the day so he could make it through the week so he could make it to the weekend, now he relished each day as if it were a gift to be enjoyed with gusto. Time and again, he lived out the tumultuous time of the Lincoln County War in his mind. He could almost see the bedrock events of the war playing in a movie reel in his mind that only he could view. He now scoffed at Young Guns as being inauthentic and riddled with errors, and looked down his nose at anyone who suggested that The Kid killed the 21 men that legend has credited him with. In short, he'd become a Billy the Kid snob and Martin relished in it. At least now he belonged to something, had passion for something. He could bore people to tears at parties (if they ever even attended a party that is) with arcane facts about the Fritz insurance policy or the amount of inventory Tunstall had ordered to open his store. While it might not win him many invites to the golf course (which he'd have to turn down since he'd never taken up the game), it would at least make him an expert in something….anything really, that could justify his existence as a functioning member of society.

Lilly sensed a change in him as well. He was more motivated, at least as it pertained to his new obsession. While so far his newfound energy hadn't translated to a raise at work or a more romantic relationship with her, Lilly at least saw a spark in Martin's eyes that had dimmed, and then gone out years ago. During several of their dinnertime conversations, he floated the idea of a romantic trip "out west" that Lilly knew was code for New Mexico. She was firmly NOT in the "Billy the Kid is my hero" camp and had zero interest in a murderer of lawmen that had died almost 140 years ago. Still, she drew some comfort that somehow Martin's addiction might someday include her, growing their bank account, and seeing more of the world than Bergen County offered.

"Can we afford all of these books Martin?" she demanded, "I mean, it seems like they're all about the exact same thing. How many of them do you really need to read?"

"Same thing?" asked Martin, incredulous that Lilly obviously hadn't been paying attention for the past two months "Every one of these books lays out key information on the story of The Kid. I want to know it all Lil, not just that BS that Hollywood feeds you. They may look similar, but every one of these authors and historians has found something slightly different than the person that came before them. One day, and I hope it's before I die, we're going to really know who Billy was…and I hope to hell I'm around when we do!"

Knowing she wouldn't make any progress in Martin's state of mind she simply handed him the box with a soft "hmmphh" and strode inside. As Martin turned his eyes to follow her, he sensed the merest hint of Lilly's head shaking in what he assumed was disgust. Martin made his way to the kitchen to carve open the package and see what historical riches lay inside. Upon examining the contents of the well packed box, Martin was satisfied that he had enough study material for the week. Carefully he picked up a volume on the Lincoln County War and thumbed through it while he poured another cup of coffee down his waiting throat. Out of the corner of his eye he caught Lilly in her jogging outfit about to go for a run.

"Hey uh, Lil" Martin began, "I've really been thinking about that vacation we talked about. How about we go to Rosario's for dinner tonight and plan something?"

While dinner and a glass of wine at Rosario's sounded wonderful to Lilly, a debate on visiting some dusty old town in the middle of New Mexico certainly did not. Lilly carefully considered the offer before responding, "Listen Martin, with your newfound excitement about Billy the Kid you've probably spent more on books in the last 2 months than our vacation would cost. I just don't think we should spend the money. We're not getting any younger and you're not making any more money than you have been." As soon as she said it, Lilly regretted it. Martin was a good man, a decent husband, and a good provider. While her life hadn't exactly turned out as intended, Lilly didn't want to hurt the man she loved and planned to spend the rest of her life with. Martin had winced visibly upon hearing her final shot and she wanted to make up for it quickly.

"I'm sorry honey, I didn't mean it like that. I know they don't appreciate you the way that they should down at the office. You've given them 17 years of your life in the same job and the best they could manage was a few cost-of-living raises. Someday they'll see what they have and pay you what you're really worth, just you see my sweet husband" Lilly gushed at Martin as forcefully as she dared.

Martin couldn't stay mad, and he secretly wanted Lilly to leave so he could start picking apart the chapters on the Army beef contracts awarded to The House of Murphy so he simply replied "Thanks babe, have a great run. Let me know about Rosario's when you get back?"

Lilly smiled at the quick fix and bounded out the door as Martin dug in for as much reading as he could get done before it was time to fertilize his lawn.

13.

"What do you think Marty?" asked Colin, "got anything for the contest Marty?"

It was another bland Monday morning at the office, and while Martin would rather be home studying up on The Kid, he had bills to pay and to Lilly's point, he had been spending a lot more money recently than he was used to. Work seemed like the logical place to be.

The contest that Colin McGlinchy was speaking of was the Parmalove Brothers Ad Agency's "safety slogan" affair. Generally, while working in an ad agency isn't as dangerous as say, crab fishing in Alaska or doing steel work on skyscrapers in New York City or Chicago without a safety belt, it still had its pitfalls. When old Alice Green slipped and fell down a flight of stairs after some young gun had spilled pickle juice after his lunchtime workout, the agency was forced to pick up the tab for her convalescence. Just weeks later, Greg Trebenlove had been hit by the company's delivery van after he darted out of the stairwell in the parking garage. While the closed circuit cameras captured him in what looked like a Spiderman pose trying to swing in front of the van, the footage was not conclusive enough to have him admitted to the psyche ward and again, the company had to foot the bill.

To counteract these injury expenses the risk management department decided a little contest was in order and offered two round trip tickets to anywhere in the continental US (coach, of course) to anyone that could come up with a new slogan for their safety campaign.

"Not yet Colin. I'd sure like to win those tickets and take Lil on a trip though. What've you got?" sighed Martin to his one friend in the office.

"Ok, ok" replied Colin impatiently as he held up his hands to build some drama, "check this out. A safe workplace is a happy workplace. Huh? Huh? What do you think Marty? Should I start working on my tan?"

Martin was amused by the young man but felt the sudden urge to yawn. Not wanting to insult him he attempted to stifle it which only caused a huge belch to permeate from his stomach instead. "Geez, I get it!" said a disappointed Colin, "It's not great, but I'm not one of these ad guys upstairs. Why don't they just ask them to do it? We're an AD AGENCY for God's sake!"

Trying to calm Colin's sudden anger Martin offered "I think they just want to get everyone involved. You never know where the next great idea might come from? And, your slogan is not bad at all Colin. I just had a big lunch, you know. I brought some leftover veal scallopini from Rosario's. You know how much they load up on the garlic"

"You really think it's ok Marty?" asked Colin hopefully.

"Hey, it's better than mine," said Martin, spreading his hands across his barren desk, "I can't even come up with anything. I guess that why I'm stuck here in quality control rather than upstairs with the big boys." Suddenly sad and feeling that maybe 17 years in one job was enough, Martin looked at Colin thoughtfully, but said nothing.

With a nod of his head, Colin walked off, satisfied that his submission might even have a chance to win. Martin stared at a blank computer screen with zero ideas and even less motivation. He wasn't required to submit an entry into the contest, but just the thought that he might convince Lilly to travel to Lincoln pushed him into action. He scanned his barren desk for ideas and spied his calculator. He had a very brief flash of inspiration and quickly typed onto his screen:

SALES + SAFETY = $UCCESS!

Satisfied that he could do no better, he emailed it to risk management and thought no more about it for the rest of the day. Judging was to take place on Wednesday and Martin held out slim hope that his slogan would better those of the guys upstairs who made in the high 6 figures and still had 2 martini lunches.

Amazingly when Wednesday arrived, Martin received an inter-office call from the head of risk management. The shrill ring of the phone shocked him from his daydream of the dusty main street of Lincoln.

"Hey Martin Teebs? This is Dana Spilcher of Risk Management. You submitted a slogan for our contest, right?" came the cheery voice on the other end of the phone.

Martin was wary, as if Colin might be putting him on but played along "Ummm…Yes, I did."

"Well, we *LOVED* it Martin!" exploded Spilcher, her enthusiasm so voluminous that it either had to be fake, or she had to be on some cocktail of powerful drugs, "It's exactly right, we *have* to keep making sales to be successful, but if we're not safe all of that profit is going to go right down the drain. This is incredible Martin. You are our winner. Congratulations!"

Martin was momentarily stunned, but recovered enough to thank the woman for her kind words. He nearly hung up the phone before she offered "Oh, we'll put your tickets in the interoffice mail. Enjoy your trip. Any idea where you might go Martin?"

Martin mind was already drifting toward the rough and tumble mountains and deserts of New Mexico as he heard himself say "I've got an idea or two, but I'll have to talk it over with my wife. I'd love to go see some old friends."

He spent the rest of the day staring at online pictures of Billy the Kid country and went so far as to put a refundable deposit on a casita at Lincoln's premier bed & breakfast Juan Patron's Place. Now, if he could only talk Lilly into it?

14.

The stark bright desert sun shone harshly through the rental car's windshield. This was sun, real sun, powerful sun, and not at all like New Jersey sun. Lilly's faux diamond encrusted bargain store sunglasses couldn't keep up and that began to irritate her.

"Did you turn the air conditioner up Martin? I'm roasting over here," she asked in an annoyed voice, although plainly aware that he already had. Their tiny 4 cylinder econo rental care simply didn't have enough power to move them down Interstate 25 South at 80 miles per hour and keep up with enough cool air to fend off the desert heat. "How hot is it outside anyway?" she added in Martin's general direction although she wasn't sure that he was even paying attention. From the moment the pilot announced they were on final approach to the Albuquerque International Sunport with Martin craning his neck to see the promised land, to this very instant, he'd been wearing a funny little half smile that Lilly might have seen on someone who's IQ might match the total of a high scoring football game. While she was satisfied that her husband was happy, she had come to New Mexico under false pretenses knowing that Martin's portrayal of their trip as a "romantic little getaway" with just a 'smattering' of Billy the Kid was far from her current, and likely future, truth. "For better or for worse," she remembered thinking, just before she gave in and agreed to the weeklong getaway to one of the country's most remote and poor states. If nothing else it would be a vacation, one that was sorely needed. If Lilly need to allow Martin to indulge his fascination with a dead boy for a few days to get the hell out of Dodge, then this was probably the best way to do it.

"The dash thermometer says 96 degrees Lil!" chirped Martin happily, "but you know those things are always set a little high." He stared contentedly out over the landscape as signs for towns like Los Lunas, Belen, and Socorro rolled by. Sensing Lilly's growing frustration along with her perspiration he offered "But you know, it's really a dry heat out here." Lilly glanced sideways, a sneer starting to form on her lips, but decided she wouldn't ruin their trip before it really got started. Finally at the exit for San Antonio, NM they escaped the high speed ribbon of asphalt and were firmly pointed to the southeast, towards Lincoln, NM.

"Won't be long now my dear" Martin said, as Lilly cast him a sideways glance that could have meant "Who cares" or perhaps "You're crazy"? The miles rolled on as the sun held high in the western sky. Passing through a huge expanse of valley, Martin took note that they were close to the Trinity Site, which stood as a memorial to the USA's first atomic bomb test in 1945. Pointing to the sign that explained the ominous history of the place, he mused, "Must have been something to be right here when they detonated an atomic bomb on American soil. I heard it was so top secret they didn't even tell any of the locals what they were doing!"

Lilly shot Martin an unbelieving look, "I'm sure they couldn't just set off an atomic bomb without allowing people to take precautions Martin. Where did you hear that?"

"I don't know Lil. For years afterwards though, people had all sorts of strange illnesses. At least, that's what I read" assured Martin. If Lilly had reservations about Lincoln, she put them aside for the moment as she tried to weather the current storm of knowledge of a nuclear test on unsuspecting people just miles from where their tiny car rolled through the majestic valley. She wondered what kind of people lived here, and if they would have even left if given the proper notice?

Carrizozo was rolled through just barely above the speed limit and both Martin and Lilly were amazed at the otherworldly look of the Valley of Fires, an ancient volcanic lava flow that preceded the small town. Far from New Jersey, Lilly decided at some point to stop fighting it and to just let their vacation happen, which immediately brightened her mood and her view of her husband. After taking note that Capitan was the burial site of Smokey the Bear they stopped to gas up at the local gas station and convenience store.

"Hey Lil, would you mind driving? I want to take some pictures as we drive into Lincoln?" Martin asked.

"Sure hon, how much farther is it" she asked. Lilly pondered saying no since she'd heard about how crazy drivers can be out in the middle of nowhere but figured this was their first and last trip to New Mexico so she could at least indulge Martin in his quest to find Billy the Kid, or whatever the dusty little town in the mountains had left of him.

Pleasantly surprised, Martin reported that they had only 10 miles or so to go before reaching his personal Nirvana and he didn't plan to miss a minute of it. Slipping into the passenger seat he grabbed his cell phone to make sure it was well charged for the onslaught of pictures he planned to take. They carefully rolled out of the station and

Lilly pointed the car east towards Lincoln, NM. and towards a date with destiny that neither of them knew they were about to have.

15.

The bland green road sign simply said "Lincoln" on it as Martin craned his neck toward the driver's side of the car, attempting to see anything except rocks, shrubs, and desert around the rock escarpment. If New Mexico was planning to create some shock and awe campaign to welcome tourists to Billy's former digs, they hadn't done it yet. As they approached the town they were met by a small scattering of buildings and then almost as if the gates of Heaven had been opened Martin was face to face with "The House", the old Murphy Dolan store that served as The Kid's jail and from where he shot his way to infamy killing both of his guards just months before being shot and killed himself by Pat Garrett in Fort Sumner.

Martin's voice rose an octave or two at the sight, "Oh my God! There it is Lil! The courthouse, the Murphy Dolan Store. Right there! Right THERE is where The Kid killed that bully Olinger, with Olinger's own shotgun!"

With a few scattered tourists walking along the edge of the roadway, Lilly acknowledged his find with an audible and disinterested, "Hmmmm" but continued to focus on the road. Martin's head was on a swivel as they drove by the Tunstall store, Wortley Hotel, and the famous Torreon', all sites Martin had seen a hundred, a thousand times online but now was in the very presence of.

"Oh, this is incredible. I can't believe that 140 years ago there was a real war here. With real men fighting and dying. I can't believe I'm…" Martin quickly thought the better of and corrected himself, "I mean we're here Lilly"

As the car slowly meandered along Lincoln's only street they neared the east edge of town before the sign for Juan Patron's Place came into view.

"This is it, I guess" said Lilly as the car slowed and glided to a stop in the crunchy gravel parking lot, "looks pretty nice huh Martin?"

Almost before the car stopped Martin jumped out of the passenger seat so he could walk the same ground that The Kid had all those years ago. While not ignoring Lilly he also didn't answer her, wanting to remember this moment, his first time in Lincoln, forever. As his feet touched the sacred earth he said, "This is God's country huh Lil?

Just look at this." speaking with tones usually reserved for church service.

"Yeah, it's nice. It's very…" Lilly paused to put the right affect on her voice so as not to bring Martin crashing to Earth "peaceful. Yeah, peaceful."

Martin wandered towards the main street looking westward back into the heart of Lincoln. While he didn't intend for anyone to hear him he clearly spoke loud enough to give Lilly some alarm. "I'm here Kid. I can't believe it. I'm here" announced Martin to the ghost of a boy long since gone. Wide eyed with wonder he spun 360 degrees around as if he had someone magically been transported to a home that he never knew he missed.

"This trip is not going to be all about Billy the Kid is it Martin?" Lilly's voice sliced in, "We're going to do things right? Like actual things together? Like we planned?"

Quickly snapping back from wherever the town had transported him he made a glove save, "Of course Lil, this is just a nice quiet place for us to get away. See" he said holding out his cell phone, "I don't even get a signal on my phone here. It's just you and I, no distractions. It's going to be great, I promise"

To cement his recovery Martin pulled Lilly in tight for a genuine hug, a move which surprised her at first, and gave her some hope that the trip might rekindle their waning love life. Already not great, it had positively fallen off the charts when Martin's obsession with Billy the Kid took hold. He spent night after night reading into the wee hours of the morning and Lilly was left to find her own means of satisfaction in an increasingly platonic relationship.

"Ok, let's check in" chirped Lilly happily slipping her purse over Martin's shoulder, as well as giving him the task of getting both of their luggage. Struggling with the trunk of the car and Lilly's oversize roller bag, he noticed his well-read copy of Bachaca's book sliding out of his carry-on bag.

"Wouldn't want you to go missing" Martin said affectionately to the book that he regarded as the singular authoritative biography of The Kid. He slipped the book gently back into his bag and joined Lilly on the porch.

16.

"Hey there! You must be the Teebs," said a buxom woman in yoga pants, an almost see thru white tank top, and a cowboy hat, "Welcome to Juan Patron's House!". Darlene Jones and her husband Dallas were the overly friendly proprietors of the historic building, running it as a bed and breakfast while Dallas pursued his dreams of being a famous actor, (no small feat to accomplish living in Lincoln, NM) and Darlene seemed to delight in getting to know her guests as well as possible.

Assuming that the women should take the lead in introductions Lilly chimed in "Hi, yes Martin and Lilly Teebs. Nice to meet you". Lilly thrust out her hand in Darlene's direction and was met with a warm smile and a firm handshake in return.

Just then a cowboy, or the best approximation of a cowboy that he could put together came bounding out of the front door. All pecs and a spectacular white smile, Dallas Jones was shod in cowboy boots, skin-tight jeans, and a checked short sleeve shirt that was at least 1 size too small for him. While he had the decency to button at least one of the shirts fasteners, it turned out it was the bottom one leaving his heaving chest and abs on display for all of Lincoln to see. When he finally spoke it was with the booming voice of a man who had been on too many auditions and not landed many roles, "Welcome to Lincoln, and welcome to the center of *THE* Lincoln County War" he proudly announced.

Dallas wrapped his arm behind Lilly's neck while Martin stared wide eyed at the spectacle. Not to be outdone Darlene slipped her arm around Martin's waist and began to guide him towards the front door. "Umm, let me get the bags Darlene" he began but Darlene quickly interjected, "Come on in silly, Dallas will get those for you later". Her firm grasp on his waist urged him towards the entrance and just as they reached the door she gave him a firm slap on the rump and said "We're gonna have a good time with y'all!".

Lilly turned with a nervous smile only to see Martin in similar circumstances, as the two hosts guided their new guests deeper and deeper into their home, and for a trip they'd hopefully remember forever.

17.

After checking in and finally arriving in their casita, Lilly slammed the door and barked "What the hell was that? Did you see what he did to me Martin?"

Not wanting to jeopardize his trip by acknowledging their overly friendly and possibly sex crazed hosts, Martin gave the best answer he could, "It's not like that Lil. People are just friendlier out here, that's all. You're used to New Jersey where no one even talks to each other."

"Friendlier? Are you kidding Martin?" Lilly shot back, "I'm not sure if that guy had a can of Red Bull in his pocket or if he was just happy to see me!"

Realizing he was losing his grip on a situation that could ruin their trip before it even got started, Martin pulled Lilly in tight and calmed her as best he could. "Don't worry Lil, we've got this whole casita to ourselves. It's like our own little love nest. This is going to be perfect. I promise."

"Well, ok then. If you're sure…" Lilly questioned as she calmed a bit at Martin's promise.

They made short work of unpacking in the cute and cozy casita remembering Dallas' instructions to return to the main house at 5pm for a delicious dinner with their other guests.

Just before 5, they made their way across the courtyard to enjoy something called green chile enchiladas that Darlene told them would be the best they'd ever have in New Mexico, and probably anywhere else.

18.

One hour later, and with a full belly, Martin stepped on to the front porch of Patron's with Lilly not far behind.

"You sure don't get Mexican food like that in New Jersey, huh Lil?" said Martin while adjusting his belt open a notch. Dressed like an out of place tourist, he wore running shoes, a pair of what appeared to be mom jeans, and a brightly colored nylon shirt that had a blend of cats and fireworks (for some strange reason) festooned all over it.

Lilly, now more calm from the 3 glasses of wine she had than from the dinner replied "I'm stuffed, but that was really good". The two took in the evening air as the quiet of the mountain valley settled in their ears. "Martin, there was a second there where something seemed weird. Did you feel it?" Lilly asked curiously. Full of enchiladas and good tidings from the trip, Martin quickly answered, "No, what do you mean? What happened?" Lilly crinkled her eyes, trying to remember the fleeting thought that she'd had while they were eating dinner. Try as she might, she couldn't reel it in. It was as if someone replaced just one frame of a movie with a completely different film, but even after you saw it, you couldn't rewind to figure out what it meant. Finally, giving up on the mental tease, she relented, "I don't know. It was probably nothing….forget it."

The town, just before sunset beckoned Martin to go exploring as all he'd seen so far were the sights on the way in, the inside of his casita, and a random flash of Darlene's boobs when she seemed to purposely drop a fork in front of Martin while serving dinner. He was chomping at the bit to see more of the tiny village he'd flown across the country to pay homage at.

"You sure you won't come for a walk with me?" he inquired of Lilly as he patted his belly.

"No, I'm beat. You go. That was a long flight, and a long drive. I think I'll stay here and take a bath. Maybe read up on some things to do tomorrow." giving Martin the assent to take on Lincoln all by himself.

Giving Lilly an enchilada laced peck on the cheek he bade her farewell and set off on an adventure that started his heart pounding. Just as he stepped off the porch Lilly teased "Have fun, and don't get into any gunfights!" Forming his thumb and forefingers into pistols, he waved them over his head and winked back at her as he walked out of sight.

Lincoln, NM is a roughly one mile long strip of asphalt with historic buildings and museums lining both sides of the street. Except for the semi trucks sometimes barreling through town, it's a quiet little place where one can get lost in their thoughts and dreams. As compared the garish tourist trap of Tombstone, Arizona, Lincoln almost seemed to be a town caught, or was it lost, in time?

In the early evening light Martin saw no one else out walking. Pulling a flyer he'd picked up in the main house from his pocket, he quickly realized that all of the museums and monument buildings were closed for the day. With a sigh he figured he'd at least get to walk to all of the historic sites in peace and quiet, while returning tomorrow to continue his research.

What had been a clear and warm night just seconds ago quickly changed as a fog or mist of sorts seemed to settle on the main street. Martin assumed that the high mountain valley would suffer some interesting weather at times, but he was unprepared for how rapidly Lincoln's weather was changing right before his weary eyes. Martin looked puzzled at the sudden onset of weather but forged on. At some points the fog was so thick he couldn't see his shoes, and he wound up veering into the road like a drunken sailor. The sharp blast of a semi horn coming directly at him from behind blew him from the road, where he tumbled into a small ditch.

Rising to check his body parts over he found nothing broken or torn, and brushed the dirt from his pants. Suddenly Martin froze in his tracks for what was a quiet, almost vacant town a moment ago had dramatically come to life in the few seconds it took him to climb out of the ditch. The fog now gone, he looked down to see Lincoln's main street covered in dirt. There seemed to be more buildings now, and men, women, children, and horses scurried about as if life had been this way for 100 years. With his mind struggling to comprehend what had happened, he approached a woman dressed in a vivid green dress of the style that would be worn in the 19th century and asked "Excuse me Miss. Is this some kind of street theater?" The woman took one look at Martin's outfit and recoiled in fear, and perhaps horror. She rushed off as Martin yelled after her "What time did this all start?!"

Clearly out of his element, and in a state of extreme confusion Martin walked into the street to find out just what the heck was going on. Passersby gave him queer looks as if *HE* was the one out of place, and not them with their clothes, hairstyles, guns, and assorted other old west paraphernalia. Looking across the street he spied the Tunstall Store that he'd seen on the way in just hours ago. For some reason it looked similar, but different. His mind locked on the few possibilities that it could. First, he could have happened into the middle of some Old Lincoln Days festival and not known about it. That didn't make sense to him because of the ease with which he booked a room, and the general vacancy of the town just a few minutes ago. Second he might have received a head injury in his fall into the ditch and this could all be a vivid dream. Martin pinched himself hard and let loose an "Oww!" before he could stop himself. Still assuming it might be a dream he slapped himself in the face as if to brace himself. The slap, hurting more than the pinch convinced him that he was indeed awake. His final thought was that somehow this whole charade might even be real, a thought which he quickly discarded for fear he might be right. He imagined a nice ,comfy padded cell somewhere as he tried to describe his rapid descent into madness by a kind, if not completely understanding therapist. Not knowing his next move, he walked toward the Tunstall store, the only building he recognized from his books.

"Whaddya need more cartridges for Chavez, you can't hit the broad side of a barn with the ones you have?" said a slender blonde-haired man to one of the men on the porch.

"I took out Rolly Brogan's eye at 50 paces with my eyes closed so I don't know what the hell you're talking about anyway Scurlock" replied the solid, squat Hispanic man.

Among general chatter from the four men who seemed to be friends, Martin heard the names French and Bowdre and it occurred to him that if he was indeed dreaming, this was one hell of an accurate dream. He could no longer deny that he was standing nearly face to face with a group of the famous Lincoln County Regulators.

As people milled around and past him, Martin slowly and carefully shuffled toward the porch of the store. Somewhere from behind a gate a big old bulldog barked at him. The dog's barking caught the ear and eye of Doc, who finally noticed the big man in the strange clothes. A warm smile spread across the man's face as he walked out into the road.

"Teebs!" shouted Scurlock to Martin who was clearly amazed that someone knew his name, "How've you been you sonofabitch!?" Martin was frozen in his steps as Doc, Charlie, Jim, and Chavez all walked toward him with smiles on their tanned faces.

"How, how do you guys know my name. Did the folks up at Juan Patron's Place put you up to this?" stammered Martin now beginning to panic that he might be losing his grip on reality.

Before Doc could answer Chavez stated emphatically "Juan ain't got no place in this fight."

Doc stepped closer and put his hand on the big man's shoulder, "What's wrong Teebs, you got the consumption or something?" he deadpanned as the rest of the Regulators howled in laughter.

Not knowing how far this game might go, Martin carefully considered his next words, "Is this some kind of street fair, or a play or something? I'm sorry guys, I'm just a little off balance with all this."

French rolled his dark eyes and retreated to the Tunstall store, mumbling something about need to fetch Billy. Before any of the men in front of him could answer his name was shrieked by a decidedly female voice coming in hard and fast from between the two buildings behind him.

"*Martin!! Martin*! You're back!" cried the deliriously happy and very pretty woman. Rosita Luna was known as the Belle of Lincoln. Clearly the most beautiful woman in the county, she was courted by all manner of rogues, vagabonds, sinners, and honest men. She however only had eyes for one man. The one man now firmly in her clutches. "Oh *mi amor*, they tell me you never come back but I knew in my heart you would" said Rosita as she smothered Martin with hugs and kisses. Rosita's warm body melded with Martin's in an exciting mix of fear and excitement. It had been so long since Lilly had grabbed Martin like she actually wanted to, that he relished in the strange feeling for a second or two.

Chavez piped in "Don't keep that woman waitin no more Teebs, cause she's been waiting a LONG time!" as the Regulators broke down in laughter again.

Martin look frantically around for an escape hatch from this reality. He half expected Lilly to be standing by the roadside laughing at him for believing in this silly fantasy. He scanned to the east and west hoping maybe another semi truck would barrel down on them and wipe this memory from his mind. All he wanted in that moment was to walk back to Patron's and climb into bed so he could sleep this off.

Rosita latched her arms around Martin's neck and pressed her body close to his. As much as he worried Lilly might somehow show up and believe he was cheating on her, it wasn't an entirely unpleasant experience. As the Regulators kept up the small talk Rosita tugged at his arm, "Come *mi amor*, those *bastardos* from Dolan will make trouble if they see us here. Come." Just as Martin was allowing himself to be led off the street, a bellowing voice of a young man cut through the din, "Teebsie! You old sonofabitch! Where you been?"

Had God himself beamed down from heaven with a corned beef and cabbage sandwich for Martin's dinner, he would not have been more surprised than to find himself standing face to face with the boy he studied for months, the face that was so familiar that it could not be mistaken, and with an air of fun and frivolity that all of the history books said belonged to him.

Martin Teebs stood arm in arm with his apparent love interest Rosita Luna, as he met for the first time ever, William H. Bonney, alias Billy the Kid.

19.

For most people, coming face to face with a legend is a once in a lifetime thing. For Martin, it was multiplied by a factor of 140 years from the time he started his day in New Jersey to the way it was finishing in New Mexico. He stared at the young man who looked almost exactly like the famous tintype. The boy couldn't have been more than 5'7" and maybe weighed 135 pounds soaking wet. He had sharp eyes and a crooked little smile which seemed to be on display at almost all times. His clothes were nothing special and it appeared that he and the rest of the Regulators had been out working as they were all appropriately pasted in dust and grime. The Kid wore a large sombrero that he tilted back to get a better look at the big man.

"Damn Teebsie, you are a sight for sore eyes. We's wonderin when you was gonna make it back." Billy's friendly laconic tone drew Martin in. The big man leaned in as if looking at a museum display, still not believing what his eyes were showing him.

"Billy? Billy the Kid" asked Martin incredulously, his eyes as wide as saucers.

"Hehe, Billy'll do jes fine around here buddy" said Billy as he looked the big man up and down, "What in the hell are you wearin Teebsie? I ain't never seen no kit like that before." Billy touched Martin's ridiculous shirt and rubbed the material between his thumb and forefinger, giving a disapproving shake of his head as a result. Rosita, tired of Martin talking shop with his buddies, urged him to come home so she could cook him a proper dinner. Between this beautiful woman begging him to come home with her, standing before the outlaw legend Billy the Kid, and the rest of the Regulators laughing at his Reeboks, Martin's world was spinning out of control. His heart was beating rapidly and he was sweating profusely. The sights, sounds, and smells of the town were making him woozy. He feared if he didn't get out of here soon, he'd pass out. After struggling for a few moments, he finally found the words to try to pull his world, and his mind, back together.

"Hey guys, this has been fun and all, but my wife's going to be waiting for me and I probably need to get going" he stated as firmly as he dared.

Ice water ran through Rosita's veins as she snapped "Your wife!?" and slapped Martin as hard as he'd ever been hit right across the face. French laughed so hard that snot shot from his nose and Chavez hit the ground laughing and holding his belly to keep from crying.

"Damn, you sure got her dander up. When the hell did you get you a wife Teebsie?" asked Billy, his smile widening and his eyes alight, daring Martin to answer the question.

All Martin could do besides watch Rosita storm off, fists clenched into balls, was to rub his cheek and stammer out a few syllables that had no chance of forming an actual word. Taking pity on his friend, Billy grabbed Martin by the shoulder and led him away from the store asking "Where are you staying, cause you sure ain't staying with Rosita tonight?" Billy laughed heartily at his own joke and his friend's misfortune.

"Um, Juan Patron's place" Martin replied weakly pointing up the street.

"C'mon amigo, I'll walk ya," said the young outlaw "things are getting bad here with those Dolan boys after they killed John. You'd think we killed one of their bosses the way they actin." Billy's cool confidence inspired Martin to start shuffling his feet back toward what he hoped was a wake-up call from this all too realistic dream.

As they made their way east along the street Martin had to ask the question he'd been dreading. The one option he'd not wanted to consider. Option number four. "Hey Billy, am I dead or something? How did this happen? How did I get here?" he asked finally, expecting the worst but hoping for the best.

"Man, the only ones going to be dead are Dolan and his boys. You ain't dead Teebsie, not yet anyway" came Billy's grinning reply.

As the two men approached a very different Patron house than Martin remembered, he turned again to the young man, "Thanks for walking me Billy. I appreciate it. I need to get some sleep, or maybe have a stiff drink or two."

"Sounds good my friend. Oh, and hey Teebsie, don't go telling Rosita bout your wife no more" laughed Billy as he turned back towards the store. Remembering he had something important to tell his friend, Billy quickly turned back "Hey, don't come out tomorrow morning less your carrying this" he said as he fished around inside his waistband and produced one of Sam Colt's finest revolvers. The 1873 bird's head shone magnificently in the setting sun, loaded with 5 live rounds and a spent shell under the hammer. He held it out to Martin butt first, tempting the big man to take it.

Martin look fascinatingly at the shiny gun for a moment before snapping to his senses, "What? No way, my wife would kill me if she sees me with that!"

Billy laughed heartily as he stuck the gun back in his waist "Ok lover boy, suit yourself. But I done told you, stop talking bout your wife less you wanna get another one across the face." He laughed again as he gently slapped the air near Martin's face and walked away into the night.

Martin staggered in the gloaming toward what he hoped was the Patron house but veered into the road. As a horse quickly galloped up on him the rider yelled "Get out of the way you idiot!" and rode off, hoping to achieve his farm just a few miles outside of Lincoln to the east ,before darkness fell. The close call knocked Martin off the road into the grass and when he came to, it was sunset in Lincoln on March 31, 2020 and the town had been completely restored to what he'd left after dinner.

Swallowing hard and shaking more dust from his clothes, he made his way past his rental car in the driveway to the casita where Lilly must surely be waiting.

20.

Carl Farber stood firmly in front of his 11th grade US history class as he'd done for many years. While Farber dreamed of fame and fortune as a youth, his studies at Bergen Community College didn't portend a future filled with private jets, bottle service, and sexy supermodels. This, this classroom filled with entitled little snots who drove cars that probably cost as much as a house was what he was left with. If they paid attention to him at all, it was only to mock what he was trying to teach them, or pretend to be listening so that they could bump up a failing grade. That thought burned in Farber as he taught the day's lesson on his most passionate subject, the Lincoln County War.

"And so was born the infamous Lincoln County War of New Mexico students. A war between merchants and ranchers, driven by the powers of the Santa Fe Ring" proclaimed Farber. Almost no one heard him because those that were awake had their noses buried in ever more expensive cell phones and tablets. The school "discouraged" usage of phones during class but didn't expressly forbid it, so Farber was left almost teaching for his own benefit.

Gritting his teeth he pressed on, "Can anyone tell me what infamous figure was born out of said war?"

One student lifted his head out of his screen and couldn't help but take the bait "Your mother?" he inquired. The class exploded in laughter as Farber turned red with anger, unsure of how long he'd spend in jail for kicking the insolent little shit's ass.

"No!" barked Farber at the suddenly alive class, "Don't you people remember anything?"

The class clown would never have survived a long life as a fish, eagerly taking the bait again, "I remember your mother from last night!" as the class howled in laughter a second time.

Farber's fists instinctively tightened and his jaw went tight but going to jail today would most certainly ruin his plans tomorrow. "Out of the Lincoln County War" he announced snapping off each word as if they were formally connected "came the notorious gunslinging, murdering punk William H. Bonney. You might remember him as

Billy the Kid"

The combination of laughter, Farber's red face, and some good old gunplay roused the video game generation kids as someone from the back of the room yelled "Billy the Kid? He was so cool!" to which others in the class murmured their assent.

"Cool?" said the disbelieving Farber, "You think killing 3 lawmen in cold blood is cool?" The class had seen their history teacher go off on tangents before and knew it was time to shut up and pretend to listen.

Not a sound cut the silence as Farber continued, "You think making a living stealing horses and cattle is cool?" Still the class sat back with no one daring to interject.

Farber's anger at the idea of The Kid as well as at his class (which he judged no better than Bonney) infuriated him. "You think sending your OWN FRIENDS TO DIE IS COOL??" he screamed into the void of 25 pimply faced suburban teens.

Finally, a student in the front row spoke up "Ok, we get it Mr. Farber. Chill dude."

Farber paced back and forth in front of the class as if a lion, deciding which one of them to eat first. "Oh, I'll chill all right" he said directly into the kid's face, "Tomorrow I leave for Lincoln, New Mexico where I'll put the final touches on my book about the REAL Billy the Kid. When I'm done the world will never look at that abject coward as a…" and here Farber deftly pulled out the air quotes "'hero' again."

Satisfied by their silence that he'd made his point, Farber strode back toward his desk muttering the word "cool" to himself while shaking his head in disgust. A pin drop could have been heard until a lone voice from the back of the room broke the silence, "Mr. Farber, you know who's still going to think Billy the Kid is cool no matter what your book says?"

Farber, intrigued, slowly turned toward the back of the room and straightened up, as if he might gain some valuable information. "Who?" he said curiously.

"Your mother!" came the reply as the class was beside itself with laughter. As if on cue the bell rang and the kids quickly filed out leaving a smoldering Farber in their wake.

21.

In the dreary light of his apartment's fluorescent bulbs, Farber packed his bag for his early morning flight to New Mexico. Among his jeans, assorted tee shirts, socks, and underwear he had decided to bring some 1878 period clothing with him. Left over from an old west reenactors group that he was kicked out of for reasons he didn't like to discuss, Farber figured that his first trip to Lincoln should be a memorable one, and looking like a local might even make him feel like one. He wasn't completely sure that the few residents that still resided in town dressed as if they were still in the Lincoln County War, but he mused that there was nothing else the town was famous for, so they surely must, at least to keep tourists coming to spend their hard-earned dollars.

Gathering up his belongings he began to make a mental list to assure he hadn't left anything behind.

"Clothes, check. Money, check. ID, check. What else am I forgetting?" he asked of himself, "Aha, plane ticket. I'm not going anywhere without this."

Farber looked around the room to make sure he didn't overlook some key item when his eyes fixated on a neat stack of papers on his tiny desk. Picking them up and making sure they were in perfect order he looked upon the manuscript as if it were a lover, "Wouldn't want to forget you my precious". Upon the title page in big, bold letters was the title:

Billy the Kid, The Coward of Lincoln County.

Farber caressed the pages with a feel he imagined a woman would like "Just a few more days of research and I'll be done." He paused before continuing, "And then Mr. Bonney, the world will know what a sniveling little pissant you REALLY were!"

He carefully placed the manuscript into a protective folder and laid it gently on top of his clothes. Just as he was about to zip the bag shut he saw one more thing to pack. He reached over to a well-worn copy of Sergio Bachaca's "The True Life of Billy the Kid" and stared at the brightly colored image on the cover. Talking to the book in a mocking tone he said, "YOU might as well come with us too. When I'm done, they're going to have to start selling you in the fiction aisle!". Farber laughed too hard at his own joke, slipping the book into the bag and zipping it up tight for the journey ahead.

22.

If Lilly Teebs suspected anything about Martin's previous night's activities, it didn't show on her face. She and Martin sat on the portal in front of their tiny casita eating a breakfast of fresh fruit, yogurt, and granola. Martin noisily slurped coffee as he looked for any hint that Lilly might know something about Billy, and especially and more dangerously, about Rosita.

"So, how was your little sightseeing expedition last night?" she finally asked between bites of melon, "Did you have fun?"

While Martin was fascinated and even a little freaked out by what he believed happened, he was not ready to label it as fun. "It was nice. I walked around to see the sights and talked to a few locals." he finally offered.

"Locals? I didn't see another soul on the street when you left." replied Lilly looking quizzically at Martin, "Well, were they nice?"

While Martin could answer any way that he chose to, he took the time to carefully reflect on his experience and determine if the men he met were actually nice to him. They seemed to like him. In fact, they seemed to almost miss him. This fact had kept Martin awake most of the night. If what he experienced was real, and he wasn't at all ready to accept that, then he must have been in Lincoln before March 31, 1878. Certainly to meet Billy and the Regulators, and definitely to woo Rosita. As he tried to keep his mind from fixating on what he and the lovely Rosita might have done together over 140 years ago he landed on an answer for Lilly. "Ummm, yeah they were ok. This one guy was pretty friendly. I guess they don't talk to many tourists is all." he finally said.

With a brief smile and flicker of acknowledgment Lilly moved onto the topic at hand, "Ok, so what do you have planned for us today? I've heard that Ruidoso has some great shopping. Oh, and did you know that Smokey the Bear is buried in Capitan?"

"I do know that" said Martin gently, remembering Billy's warning to stay indoors this morning, "Lil, maybe we could just take in the sights from the porch this morning."

Lilly's eyes glazed over and rolled back into her head. "I want to do things Martin, see things. I don't want to be stuck all week in this dusty little town." Unsure of how to play his next move Martin sat back and waited for the next salvo. "I'll tell you what, I'm going to take a shower. If you want some time to watch the cars rust or the paint dry or whatever else it is they do for fun in this place, now's your chance" she snapped back at him, pointing out towards the road. Knowing that nothing he said would make the moment better, he wisely sat back in his chair and gave her a thin smile as she turned and walked inside.

With a belly full of food and coffee, Martin focused his attention on why it was so important for him to stay off of Lincoln's main street this morning. Picking up Bachaca's book he thumbed through the pages. "April first, April first", he murmured to no one, "why does that sound so familiar?" Scanning the pages, he came across the chapter that talked about the killing of Sheriff William Brady at the hands of Billy and other Regulators. His index finger wandered furiously across the page until he came to the date of the deed.

April 1, 1878

Had Martin stayed overnight in the past, he would have been a witness to Brady's murder. That's the reason Billy warned him about staying inside. Martin felt a warm friendly feeling for the young outlaw, who obviously didn't want him to have anything to do with something as heinous as killing an officer of the law. It suddenly dawned on him that he was free to go about Lincoln's main street as he pleased today since the year was 2020 and the danger of being mixed up in Brady's murder was more than 140 years past due. His biggest danger that morning might be getting a blister from walking to the courthouse and back.

With a flash of joy he rose from his seat. Now, he could make everything right with Lilly, and take her wherever she deemed to be not a dusty old tourist trap. Billy had somehow assumed that Martin would still be in 1878 and had no idea that he'd jump more than a century away from this morning's bloodbath. As he reached for the screen door he stubbed his foot on the boot scraper that he had never noticed until now. Falling forward he caught himself just as his forehead whacked the door frame with a loud and painful "thump".

23

Martin was sure he hadn't blacked out but coupled with his two falls from the night before, this added skull bumping proved that Lincoln was now as it was in 1878, a very dangerous town. Through slightly fuzzy vision he reached down to where he dropped Bachaca's book. Martin reached up to his forehead to feel a slight lump rapidly forming, but thankfully, no blood. As he rose he quickly noticed the same misty haze had engulfed the town from the night before. Confused, he walked off the porch as three men walked down Lincoln's main street, again covered in dirt. The figure in the center was unmistakable to Martin as he had seen his picture hundreds of times, Sheriff William Brady.

"Oh no, no, no Billy" said Martin quickly under his breath, understanding what was about to happen "Don't do this. They're going to want to hang you for this!"

Among the many casualties and indictments that were byproducts of the Lincoln County War, only Billy would stand trial for this crime some 3 years later, and would be found guilty and sentenced to hang. If Martin could somehow reach the Tunstall store before Brady maybe he could reason with the boys and talk them out of the foolhardy plan? Not withstanding the fact that he was about to attempt to change history, his affection for his new friend urged him into the street. Brady, Hindman, and Matthews all strode confidently to the west as Martin searched for a way to get in front of them. At each spot where he thought he might be able to get in front of the lawmen, he froze, not knowing if he had a history with Brady, and what might happen to him if he did. If Billy and the boys knew him well, then Brady, Dolan, and others might too? Taking shelter behind a small barn he saw Brady stop off to talk to a woman as his deputies continued on towards the courthouse. As Brady tipped his hat and hurried back to his men, Martin looked for the Hail Mary that would land him at the Regulators feet moments before Brady would arrive, but none was forthcoming. The battlefield lines had been drawn and Martin was apparently stuck in the bleachers.

Just seconds before Billy and friends would cut loose Martin could wait no more. Ration and reason were gone. He wasn't in 2020, he was right here in 1878 at the epicenter of the war. If he didn't take action, who would? Reasoning with himself that he had no other choice he ran into the street behind the lawmen and screamed as loud as his lungs would allow, "Billy…NO!"

In the blink of an eye, Brady drew his revolver and wheeled around to see the figure of a large man diving into the grass. Something flew from the man's hand into the brush as he went down. Almost simultaneously The Regulators rose from behind a corral wall at the Tunstall store and let loose with a furious fusillade of fire that shredded Brady and dropped him where he stood. Hindman was hit in the upper chest and leg and staggered back up the street from where he came. A cool calculating Doc Scurlock walked slowly into the center of the street, took aim with his Winchester, and with one shot put Hindman out of his misery.

Somewhere in the haze of powder and smoke, Billy Matthews made a run for it and parked himself behind a wall on the south side of the street. Stunned but unhurt he quietly took the scene in as Big Jim French and Billy Bonney raced to Brady's body.

"Get the papers!" yelled Billy "Brady's gotta have em". French rifled though the pockets of the dead Sheriff and came up with nothing. "They ain't here Billy" said a breathless French, "We ought to get outta here, it's gonna get hot right quick!"

True to his prediction, townspeople had begun to peek from their doors and windows, as a few brave souls ventured into the street to see their Sheriff, now shot to pieces.

"This street is ours!" shouted Chavez gleefully, nudging Brady with his boot tip as he arrived. A small pool of blood leaked out from Brady's chest as French looked up, wondering what to do next? Billy leaned over and picked up Brady's Winchester. "You owed me one you son of a bitch, so consider this payback." he taunted the corpse. As the boys worked their way back toward the coral, Billy caught sight of movement in the grass to the east. Catching sight of the strange footwear he'd seen on only one person before, Billy walked over as Martin frantically struggled to his feet.

"Teebsie!" exclaimed Billy, no less cheery than if he'd just won a game of monte "You don't listen so good. I done told you not to come out here this morning."

Martin stared at the boy's face, unsure what to say. That Billy could be so cheery after just murdering two men made his blood run cold. Nothing in his library of Billy the Kid books, or the movies he'd seen could have prepared him for this. Among the various historian and reenactor groups that Martin had found online, many in 2020 were fond of saying they were "born in the wrong century" and "would love to live in the old west". Some even professed how they would "gladly ride with The Kid" if given the chance. Martin wondered to himself how many of them were willing to face the bloody reality lying in the street just few yards from him. Not many, he silently decided to himself.

"You killed him!" stammered Martin, "Brady's dead!"

Cool as a cucumber Billy replied easily, "Awwww, Brady wasn't gonna live much longer anyway. None of them Dolan boys is."

Martin stared in disbelief at Billy as he saw a small trail of blood, Brady's blood, trailing down the stock of the Winchester that Billy had taken from him.

From behind the wall Matthews allowed himself a peek around the corner. He saw Bonney talking to a large man that he'd had a run in with once before. "God damn you Bonney!" he whispered under his breath, catching sight of his boss's body crumpled just behind him. Matthews pulled back behind the wall, took two deep breaths and in one smooth motion, cocked his own Winchester, swung around the corner of the wall and shot Bonney in his right hip.

"Ahhhh!" screamed Billy "Dammit, that hurts!" Brady's rifle dropped at Martin's feet as the young man fell to his knees in pain. In all of his life, well at least his life in 2020, Martin Teebs had never so much as handled a firearm of any type, yet in the moment he reached down and grabbed the rifle. Martin saw a head briefly appear across the street from behind the wall, surmising this must be the person who shot his friend. As if he'd done it a thousand times before, he chambered a round, shouldered, and fired the rifle putting a .45 slug right between the eyes of Deputy Billy Matthews.

Matthews fell dead, his life over before his head hit the ground. The slug blew out the back of his skull, and bits of brain and bone lay spattered around his head, almost giving a halo effect. If Billy Matthews was indeed an angel, Martin Teebs had sent him to be with his own kind.

Martin, as if he'd been in another body, snapped back to reality dropping the rifle in front of him. "Oh my God!" he cried "what did I do?" He stared at his hands as if they were aliens, with some mind of their own.

Billy struggled to his feet, still obviously in pain. "You mighta just saved my life Teebsie"

Martin, in obvious distress paced back and forth in the grass. "Oh no, I can't believe this. What the hell just happened here?" he implored of himself, the memory of Matthews brains exiting his head still fresh in his mind.

"Teebsie, we should get you outta here" said a concerned Billy "You just killed a lawman, and when you kill a lawman….."

Martin didn't allow Billy to finish his thought ,"You HANG, right Billy??" yelled Martin, his hands going to his neck as if to pull off a rough hangman's noose.

"Yeah, you hang compadre. C'mon, let's get you off the street." said Billy as he guided the bigger, older man by the shoulder back toward Juan Patron's home.

The two men shuffled up the street, one out of physical necessity and one out of mental depravity. For a long moment no one spoke. Martin couldn't think of anything to say. He wondered what it felt like to be hung. Did your neck snap right away or did you swing for a while, your failing vision watching onlookers gleefully cheer your demise? The thought made a bitter bile rise in his throat and for a moment he felt he might throw up.

Billy finally spoke "Listen Teebsie, I like you. We all do, but you's gonna have to leave Lincoln today. You hear? They ain't gonna let this go and I can't be responsible for my friend getting hurt. You hear me?"

The words "my friend" disarmed Martin. It was almost as if they had grown roots so far down in his soul that he didn't know they existed until now. Billy *was* his friend, he could feel it. How it happened, and what bigger part Martin might have taken in this war, he had no idea, but he knew it to be so. While he was revulsed by how easily the boy took life, he felt a kinship that he'd never felt with another man. Tiny fragments of memories floated around Martin's brain. He couldn't form one complete thought and they eluded him as he tried to, but something told him that this place, this boy, this war were in his past, and his future. A tear started to form in his eye.

"I know Billy. I need to go" was all the big man could muster before the stinging in his eyes proved too much to continue.

"Listen up Teebsie, get on out today. Get that wife of yours and leave Lincoln. Head back to…" Billy paused while he smiled, looking at Martin' ridiculous clothing "wherever the hell it is you come from." Billy finished with a laugh as he dusted some mud off Martin's shirt. "Don't you come back no more till you hear this war's over, you understand amigo?"

Martin's glassy eyes looked to the west as if in a trance. Somewhere down there the good citizens of Lincoln were scooping up what was left of their sheriff and wondering just who was going to restore law and order to their tiny hamlet. "I understand Billy. I got it. Thanks" murmured Martin as his friend turned to head back to the killing fields.

Martin watched Billy hobble away and just before he was out of earshot the boy offered, "Hey Teebsie! Don't go telling your wife bout Rosita neither. Ain't no sense having two woman who want to smack you!" Billy's lighthearted laughter filled the street as he walked farther away. While Martin tried to make sense of what happened, a hazy fog rolled in. As he crossed the road it began to thin, and as it dissipated he found himself once more in 2020 and walking towards his casita. Lilly was surely showered and waiting for him, never knowing her husband was now a murderer, a wanted man, and most likely an adulterer. Well, he reasoned, at least he'd have something to talk about at the dinner parties they never seemed to throw back home in New Jersey.

24

Finding the casita vacant, Martin made his way towards the main house. With the remnants of this morning's breakfast threatening to reappear at any moment, he replayed over and over the sight of Matthew's brains splattering out of the extra large hole that Martin had installed into the back of his skull. Still incredulous at what had just happened, and covered in a cold sticky sweat, the big man made his way onto the portal and into the main living area.

"Martin!" exclaimed Lilly and Darlene simultaneously, "What on earth happened to you? You look like you've seen a ghost!".

Unaware of how shaky he looked, Martin managed a peek in the mirror just around the corner in the main hallway. He had to admit, he did look like he'd seen a ghost. He ruefully remembered that he had probably just made one out of Billy Matthews too.

"I'm, I'm fine" he said unconvincingly, "I just tripped on the side of the road"

Lilly stared at him with worry while Darlene rubbed his shoulders. Before he could ask, Darlene offered "Let me get you a glass of water" and she disappeared into the kitchen.

"I was just telling the ladies about old Lincoln, and the war" offered Dallas who graciously had buttoned 2 buttons on his much too tight shirt this morning, "This street right outside was known as the deadliest street in America at the time. You can't imagine how many guys had their brains blown out right out here."

The thought and accompanying visual made Martin retch and he staggered to find a wall to rest against. Just then Darlene returned with a tall glass of water. Taking the glass in his shaky hand, Martin looked at it as though it might be a bad idea to drink it, but in one long slug he downed the entire thing, regretting it instantly.

"You really don't look too good" said Darlene with genuine concern, "would you like to sit down?"

"Sure" was all Martin could offer as he cautiously made his way to a big armchair, trying all the while to keep the contents of his stomach in place.

"So, these are the most well-known characters of the Lincoln County War" proclaimed Dallas, sweeping his hand across the wall lined with very somber looking people in somber looking poses. "This here is John Tunstall. You might say he's the reason this whole war got started. This stout fellow is Sheriff William Brady, gunned down by The Kid and some of his buddies. A lot of people think Brady deserved it, but assassinating a lawman from ambush is just wrong, don't you think Martin?"

Staring at the pictures, it was as if the men in them beckoned for Martin to answer. "Brady was a drunken prick. I'm not shedding any tears for him!" exclaimed Martin, suddenly startled by his own words. Martin looked apologetically at Lilly while she stared back in both amazement and disgust.

"Well now, that's one guy who's not on team Brady" joked Dallas, shaking his head in Martin's direction, "so, moving on."

Darlene slid across Lilly's lap to reach the picture behind her, her hips residing longer than needed on top of Lilly's dark blue yoga pants. She pointed to a beautiful woman sitting on a step holding a young baby. The woman's eyes were distant and hollow as if she were waiting for something, for someone that might never arrive. "This pretty little thing here is Rosita Luna, the Belle of Lincoln." said Darlene

"The most beautiful woman in the entire county, or so they said" added Dallas quickly.

"And that's her baby Martin Jr." said Darlene. Just as the words left her mouth she was caught by the irony. "Oh! Look at that" she said absently smiling at Martin, "what a coincidence?"

Lilly looked strangely at Darlene and then at Martin. Martin tried his best to offer a joking smile that came off as nervous. Regardless, Lilly's attention had waned and she was hoping to wrap up the history lesson and get on the road for some shopping and sightseeing. Just as she was about to suggest it, Dallas rushed in, "She never married… and no one ever knew who the father was."

Martin clearly and quickly understood the implications of what he'd just heard. He

DID have a relationship with Rosita. He DID get her pregnant, and somehow he did NOT wind up marrying her. With his world slowly beginning to spin out of control, and with cold sweat pouring from his forehead he stumbled from his chair towards the hallway.

"Martin!" exclaimed Lilly "are you all right?"

"I just…..I just…." Martin could not finish the sentence as he pressed his forehead on the cool wood paneling. The cooling effect and keeping his eyes closed seemed to steady the big man. After a minute he opened his eyes and was face to face with another historical photo, this one taken a few days after Brady's murder. Martin instantly recognized the men in it, since he'd left them only a few minutes earlier. As he peered into their distant faces Darlene came scooting in to check on him. "Oh," she said, "this one was taken right after the fight at Blazer's Mills. Buckshot Roberts got Dick Brewer in that one but The Kid barely got a scratch!".

Martin looked closely and carefully at his friend in the tiny tintype when something caught his eye. Closer and closer he looked into Billy's right hand. If God himself landed in this hallway and clapped Martin on the back he wouldn't have been more surprised than to see his copy of Sergio Bachaca's well worn book in Billy's hand, in a photo taken 140 years ago. A wave of nausea swept over the big man as he remembered the book flying from his grasp the moment Brady was shot. Billy must have found it. Martin mind played on a hundred scenarios at the same time but all coming back to the same one. He fucked up, royally. And now, the past and future might be changed. His stomach, tired of fighting the inevitable, finally let loose and sprayed his breakfast all over the wall and floor. Martin mumbled to himself "What have I done? Oh my God, what have I done?"

"You just chucked all over my new wood floor Martin, that's what you've done" came the matter of fact reply from a dismayed Dallas Jones.

25

Carl Farber sat back in his tiny seat as the plane glided majestically through Tijeras Canyon, slicing its way toward the Albuquerque Sunport. Farber had spent the past two hours dodging the cough and spittle of the way-too-big to be a lap child kid seated happily on his mother's substantial thighs. As the kid hacked again and again like a miniature Doc Holliday, Farber craned his neck to the side, hoping to see The Land of Enchantment for the first time. With a teacher's salary, vacations were hard to come by, but he'd been saving for 2 years to take this one. This was to be his crowning moment. After landing in Albuquerque, he'd take the cheapest rental car he could find and head south on I-25 towards Lincoln County. A three hour drive, if all went well, should deliver him to the promised land. Farber's dreams of literary immortality were just weeks away as this trip would allow him the time and vision to put the finishing touches on his Billy the Kid tome. Somewhere deep in his brain, he saw the families of Pat Garrett, Bob Olinger, J.W. Bell, and William Brady reaching out to him with heartfelt appreciation for finally stamping out the "Robin Hood" legend of Bonney and portraying him for what he rightfully was, a murdering coward. "It's nothing, my friends, just telling the truth." whispered Farber to his imaginary audience in the packed plane.

"What? What did you say to my little angel?" demanded the mother of the diminutive Doc.

Caught off guard Farber realized he'd been talking out loud and quickly covered himself "Oh, nothing ma'am. My apologies. I was just rehearsing for an upcoming speech."

With a frown, the mother turned away as her baby blasted one last salvo at Farber before the plane gracefully touched down in New Mexico Territory.

26

"Come on Lil!" implored Martin as he hastily threw his rumpled clothes into his suitcase.

Assuming that Martin had contracted some sort of virus, Lilly suggested they stay in the casita that day, allowing him some time to recover. Martin however, had visions of being tracked, cornered, and shot like a mangy dog on his mind. Could Brady's deputies travel forward in time and drag him back to 1878? Were they out there right now fighting through some space/time continuum? Would hanging in 1878 eliminate any trace of him in 2020? These questions played heavily on Martin's mind as he realized his only option was to get out of, and away from, Lincoln as soon as humanly possible.

"I've seen everything I need to see here, it's just a dusty old town just like you said Lil" the words sputtered from Martin lips in manic fashion. Lilly stared at her husband as if he'd gone insane. Looking up at her as she shoved clothes both dirty and clean deeper into his bag, he sputtered, "You were right all along!"

Finally, having had enough Lilly shot back "Martin! What's going on? This trip was YOUR idea. Now you want to just up and leave after one day? This is insanity!"

Martin ignored his wife's missive and quickly zipped his bag closed. Seeing that Lilly was moving at a far slower pace than he imagined the hangman would work at, he flung clothes into her bag with abandon and scanned the room to see if he'd missed anything that would leave behind any trail that a lawman could follow.

"Let's go Lil. I've had enough. This entire trip has been a huge mistake!"

Nervous at the frantic look in her husband's eyes, Lilly fought no more and slowly dragged her suitcase off the bed and onto the floor. Martin was already out the door, holding it open for her, making it clear that the time to leave was *now*.

"Alright, alright, don't rush me Martin" said Lilly sounding more than a little annoyed, "I don't know what happened to you out there but don't take it out on me!"

As they rushed to their rental car, Lilly caught sight of Dallas in the main house window. He gave her a questioning look as they frantically made their way to the trunk of the car. Martin thrust his hands into his pants pocket, fishing around for something he obviously could not find.

"Dammit!! I left the keys inside. Wait. Here." Martin commanded Lilly as he sprinted for the casita.

Martin flung the door open, and looked furiously around the tiny house, but the keys were nowhere to be seen. He quickly remembered emptying his pockets while looking for a tissue after desecrating the Jones's floor with his vomit. He hastily made his way towards the main house.

Stepping inside, the big man made sure to avoid eye contact with the Blazer's Mills picture. The impact of seeing Billy holding the book once was enough to burn it into his memory forever anyway. He scoured the living room, searching couch cushions and chairs before catching a metallic glint on a small side table. Just as he scooped up the keys his eyes were drawn to the picture of Rosita and Martin Jr. If anything, childbirth had only made the woman more beautiful. Her gaze pierced Martin as he could not tear his glance away from her haunting, vacant eyes. Was this *really* his son? What year was the picture from? It was obvious that somehow, he must have gone back in time at least one more time to procreate little Martin Jr. That thought wasn't entirely unpleasant even juxtaposed with his legally married wife waiting for him just a few yards away.

Martin allowed his gaze to linger on Rosita for a few more moments. Now that Bachaca's book was in Billy's hands, maybe this part of history would be changed too? Maybe there would be no Jr., no more trips back in time, and no more of the lovely Rosita? Martin was on the verge of the experience of a lifetime, and he'd most likely thrown it away just like he'd tossed away that damned book. The thought of that possibility made him a little sad. He reached up with his index finger and traced the outline of Rosita's face while he murmured to himself "Martin Jr, huh?" Just then he was startled by a voice coming from behind him.

"Excuse me, is this where we check in?" said a sultry female voice. Martin turned around and nearly passed out when he saw the unmistakable face and form of Rosita

Luna, the Belle of Lincoln smiling brightly at him. Wearing a form fitting fuschia dress, way-too-high for Lincoln heels, and a pair of aviator sunglasses she was all sex, seduction, and sin rolled into one. If anyone was going to come from the past to fetch him, Martin was momentarily thrilled it would be her.

"Rosita!" cried out Martin before he could stop himself. The young woman, pulling her sunglass down for a better view, smiled with a look of confusion on her face. "Excuse me? Did you say Rosita?" she replied. In a classic deer in the headlights moment, Martin didn't know how to respond. Was this a test? Should he wait for her to wink, or throw herself into his arms as she'd done the night before? Maybe she really didn't recognize him? As he stared incredulously at her, she finally extended a long slender hand. "I'm Trish. My husband and I are staying here for a few days. He's into some silly Billy the Kid thing and this was the only way to get him to shut up about it!" she said with a little laugh as Martin carefully shook her hand. "Martin. Um, Martin Teebs. My wife and I are staying here too. It's kind of a work thing, you know." Martin lied.

Trish smiled brightly but if she truly was Rosita, or a modern-day version of her who was also flipping back and forth in time, she betrayed none of that knowledge.

"Well Martin Teebs, it's nice to meet you. I guess I'll see you around" she said as she slipped her hand slowly from his and turned towards the kitchen from where Dallas and Darlene were finally making an appearance. Martin played on her every feature. Could this really be his long lost love? Was she simply a modern day doppelganger? This woman showed no proclivity towards running up to him and throwing her arms around him, no hint that she might want him to father her child. In fact, other than her amazing resemblance to the real Rosita Luna, this woman treated Martin just as every other woman he'd ever met (except Lilly) did…as if he were almost invisible. Fascinated, Martin's nerves began to calm and he decided he should stick around for awhile to see if Trish was merely playing it cool or if she was a heartbreaking historical coincidence.

"Son of a bitch." said Martin as he slowly walked out to the car to explain to Lilly that he had only been kidding, and that he couldn't wait to continue their vacation right here in old Lincoln town.

27

"Welcome To Lincoln"

Farber slowly picked his way down Route 380 eastbound as he made the final approach to the town he'd seen so many times in books, pictures, and movies. The enormity of it took his breath away as he swung around a rocky outcropping and entered Lincoln proper. A few lazy tourists lagged in the middle of the street but for once, Farber didn't feel the need to lecture them on their stupidity. Taking in the old courthouse, he felt strangely at home in this place that he'd never been before.

As he looked for a place to park his econo rental care, he felt no need to stifle the thought that had become words and was about to exit his lips.

"I'm here Kid. I'm really here....you lousy murdering little punk"....

28

"I'm really glad you two decided to stay Martin" chirped Dallas with a little wink, obviously happy to have his rooms full, "Hey, what the hell just went on anyway?"

Martin sat quietly at the kitchen table as Dallas whipped up his famous banana bread for his guests. Since Trish had appeared and just as quickly disappeared, the big man hung around the main house to see if he could get a glimpse of her, to see if there was even the tiniest spark of recognition in her eyes.

"Oh nothing, just a misunderstanding," Martin lied, "I thought Lilly wanted to leave because I hadn't been feeling well. She's always so protective and I didn't want her worrying about me."

"Well, whatever happened, I'm glad you're both here." offered Dallas as he swirled the last of 4 overripe bananas into the batter.

"Thanks Dallas, I'm gonna go find her now, but I'll be looking forward to a piece of that bread when it's done." said Martin with a devilish smile. The big man was no stranger to eating, and even less of a stranger to sweets.

Dallas didn't turn to watch Martin leave but quickly offered, "Check your bedroom." a remark which made Martin snap his head around trying to figure out how Dallas could possibly know that.

"Ummm, yeah. Ok, I will." was all Martin could muster as he slipped out the front door and headed a few steps away to their casita. Martin didn't in fact find Lilly in the bedroom, but found her sitting quietly on the portal, a look of amusement spreading across her face as her husband climbed the steps toward her.

"So, we're staying? Ok then, that was a quick turnaround. What would you like to do this afternoon honey?" she said as if waiting for an answer she didn't want to hear.

"Well, you wanted to go to Ruidoso right? Let's do that. Maybe we can have lunch and you can do some shopping." replied Martin. Lilly was happily surprised by the offer and decided to take him up on it before he changed his mind. "Ok! Let's go, I'll just grab my purse." she said and without another word scooted into the living room of the casita. Within seconds she was back, beaming from ear to ear about finally getting out of Lincoln. Martin was relatively happy as well, knowing that a happy wife did indeed lead to a happy life. As they strolled to the car he noticed that Lilly's ponytail was pushed to the side and flattened out as if she'd be laying in bed on it, but decided against saying anything so as not to spoil the cheerful mood the had both found themselves enjoying. After all, with the morning he'd experienced, how could he fault Lilly for taking a little catnap?

29

The night came easily to Lincoln with large splatters of clouds streaming across a gold and red sunset. The town, normally quiet even during peak times, was positively silent as a cheap rental car drove slowly out of town, heading west towards Capitan. It's occupant probably couldn't afford one of the pricier hotels or B&Bs in Lincoln and so would make the ten mile drive to the Smokey the Bear motel which would offer clean rooms, HBO, and free coffee to anyone lucky enough to overnight with them.

As the car cleared Lincoln proper, the sun burned one last hole in the clouds, pouring the last vestiges of light on the town that time seemed to have forgotten.

30

Martin munched heartily on his third slice of banana bread of the morning. As the crumbs collected on the sides of his mouth and then splattered on his pants, Lilly scanned Lincoln's main street. As best as she could tell, not only were she and Martin the only two people awake, but they might be the only two people left in town on this clear, cool mountain morning.

"Thanks for a great afternoon yesterday Martin. That was really a nice time." Lilly's sincerity had always only been matched by her sarcasm but this time Martin could tell she meant it.

"Of course my sweet. Ruidoso is a cool little town, and those enchiladas!" Martin knew that commenting on food was always a safe bet when he was about to launch a potentially controversial conversation. Carefully choosing his words, he inquired, "So, what would you like to do today Lilly?" By opening up a veritable Pandora's box of options, things might not go the way Martin wanted them to, but nothing ventured, nothing gained. He was like a negotiator that didn't want to throw his best price (or any price) out there first, wondering if his mark might possibly want to pay more than he even imagined?

"Well, there must be somewhere other than Ruidoso to drive to. You're the tour guide, what else is there to see?" Lilly's refusal to decide gave Martin a cause to pause, thinking Lilly might be laying some sort of trap.

"Oh, so much Lil. San Patricio, Hondo, Portales, Fort Sumner…the list goes on and on." he said truthfully.

"Let me guess, they were all Billy the Kid's hangouts, right?" responded Lilly with just a bit of condescension.

"Well, yeah," Martin said almost defensively, "but they have great scenery *and* great history. Maybe while we're out we can find some souvenirs for our friends back in New Jersey?"

"You think *anyone* in New Jersey other than you cares about this place Martin?" she said, immediately regretting the tone. After all, she didn't want to hurt Martin, but his erratic behavior since the trip began was worrying her. She'd have been just as happy to have left on April 1st rather than stay more days in a place she cared nothing about. But she loved her husband enough to let him have his playtime….at least just this once. Thinking the better of her answer she smiled brightly at Martin and said "You know what? You're right, let's go! You're the captain and I trust your judgment. Take me to see some stuff!"

Relieved that he'd at least get more time in the Kid's neighborhood, Martin smiled warmly as he shoved one last slice of banana bread in his pie hole. Lilly disappeared into the casita to get dressed and for a moment, all was right with his world again.

31

Carl Farber rose from his bed at the Smokey the Bear Motel and stretched his stiff and achy back. "Grrrunnpphhhh!" he exclaimed. While the motel's price suited his budget, the rock hard bed, musty sheets, and brown water that passed as coffee didn't suit him at all. On his meager teacher's salary, it was the best he could afford however and so he vowed not to complain. Besides, with no one to travel with, who possibly could have listened?

Rifling through his bag, he pulled out his old west reenactor clothes. As best he could, he had cobbled together an outfit that wouldn't embarrass a real 1880's cowboy too badly by visiting thrift stores and resale shops. Figuring that he might as well look the part of a successful old west author, he slid the dusty clothes on as he sat on the corner of the bed.

This wasn't the life Farber had expected when he was younger. He had fallen in love with school at a young age, which coincided with the time he fell in love with his 3rd grade teacher Mrs. Spence. She'd come to school with her huge breasts and swollen hips all tucked into too tight jeans and sweaters and it never failed to give little Farber a big Farber. He fantasized about her making him stay after school and then confessing her love to him, a boy of only 10 years old. Day after day he waited for her to give him the sign, but his wait was in vain and the sign never came. Nevertheless, the idea of teaching others things that he knew fascinated him and as he entered high school he knew that he wanted to be a university professor. He'd seen enough movies to know that these distinguished professors made tons of dough and had pretty coeds throwing themselves at their teachers. This idea suited Farber to a tee. As he graduated high school and entered college however, Farber's single mindedness began to fade and he couldn't imagine another 4 years of school to pursue his doctorate. Graduating squarely in the middle of his class, he decided that teaching high school wasn't all that bad of an idea. While there wouldn't be any nubile coeds around, there HAD to be a few 18 year old girls that would at least stroke his ego.

None of this he was living had turned out the way Farber intended. He was a loner, in a crappy job, in a crappy town. He had crappy clothes in his crappy apartment in which he ate crappy food. When he could afford to travel he could only book himself at crappy motels where he was always alone because he couldn't even claim to have crappy friends....or any friends, for that matter.

No, by this point in Farber's life he had almost nothing except a deep hatred for Billy the Kid, and a burning desire to set the record straight once and for all. He saw himself as some sort of avenging angel, fixing history's mistakes, and making himself a minor celebrity in the process.

"Where are my boots?" he mumbled to the badly stained carpet, "There you are. Ok, let's get ready to head back to Lincoln and finish this book up." Slipping the ragged boots on his feet he began to hum a few bars of 'These Boots Are Made For Walking' and laughed to himself at the joke. Gathering up the rest of his belongings, he scooped up the car key on the desk, took a last sip of the now lukewarm brown water, and headed out to his cheap rental car for the ten mile drive back to old Lincoln town.

32

Martin and Lilly sat on the portal, protected from the warm afternoon sun. Having arrived back from their excursion with no sight of Trish, Martin planned his escape into town to see if he could find her, or any trace of Rosita.

"That was a nice drive hun, thanks. Hope you had a good time." he cautiously offered.

Lilly seemed relaxed and in one of her better moods, offering him only a smile in reply.

"So….I was thinking I might take a little more time looking around town again this afternoon. Would that be ok with you?" his eyes avoided meeting hers until the final word was spoken. If Lilly was going to roll her eyes at him again, he didn't want to see it.

"Sure, why not?" she said gently with a shrug, "After all, this is our first and last trip out here so you might as well get it all out of your system."

Martin head snapped to attention as if he'd received an electric shock, "Last trip? What do you mean?"

Primed to end this conversation once and for all Lilly jumped in with both barrels blazing, "You don't really think we're coming back here, do you?" Met only with Martin's blank stare she continued, "I mean, I've indulged your little obsession here, but this isn't my idea of a vacation Martin."

Martin began to whine a little, "But I love this place, I feel so at home here"

"You mean *THIS* place?" she said mockingly, "This place that you were ready to run away from a couple of days ago? There's nothing here Martin. You've seen it all. Billy the Kid's been dead for what, 140 years? Get over it Martin, he's not coming back and neither are we!"

And with that, the air went out of Martin as if he were a balloon that had just been stuck with a safety pin. Sure, Billy wasn't coming back to Martin's time, but he was bound to see the young outlaw again, wasn't he? They were friends, pals, and you don't just abandon your pals. For the first time Martin wondered if his fate was somehow to live out the rest of his natural life in 1878 Lincoln, rather than 2020 Waldwick? He sat there, defeated, knowing he had an entire other life in some other time frame, or dimension and it appeared he'd never get back to it. He shrugged his shoulders and sighed heavily.

When he finally spoke it was as if coming from a man condemned, "Ok fine. Can I at least get a couple of hours to look around? Can I just get that?" Lilly knew when she'd pushed him too far and he was dangerously close to the edge now.

"Sure, go for it Martin. Have some fun" she relented.

Not wanting to be followed and have his alternate life possibly discovered he asked, "Thanks. What are you going to do?"

Before Lilly could answer she saw the strong frame of Dallas Jones appear in the main house window. He gazed out at her with a big smile. Suddenly Lilly didn't need to find something to keep her busy while her husband gallivanted around some ghost town. "Oh, I'll stay busy." she said with a smile as she kissed Martin on the cheek and vanished into the tiny casita.

33

Knowing his time was limited, Martin hastily made his way onto main street and began walking toward the center of town. Judging the risks, he decided that he would try to go back in time once again, to talk to Rosita and more importantly, to get his book back from Billy. The problem was, he had no idea how he'd gone back before and seemingly, had no control over where and when it would happen again. Standing to the side of the road he felt a tension headache coming on. Martin Teebs had been known for nothing his entire life. Now, if he couldn't track down Billy and get Bachaca's book back, his name would forever go down in history as the moron who gave Billy the Kid the knowledge to avoid his own death. He began to rub his head, quickly feeling the remnants of the knot he got when hitting his head on the door frame two days earlier.

"That's it!" he exclaimed, "Every time I fall or hit my head, I wind up back in 1878!"

Martin's momentary excitement faded as the prospect and pain of running headfirst into a wall entered his mind. Not ready to try something so dramatic, he gave himself a few slaps in the head with predictably, no result. Looking around he saw a telephone pole that he brushed by with his shoulder, yet still no result. Martin tried increasingly violent self harm in an attempt to knock himself back in time but the only thing he accomplished was to be beating the crap out of himself. The big man checked his watch, "One hour gone. Dammit!" he exclaimed knowing he was running out of time. He stood on the side of the road spinning in circles until he fell over from dizziness yet still, no trip back in time. Lilly's words echoed in his ears "last trip" "never again" and "your obsession" as Martin nearly burst out in tears, realizing he had absolutely no control over how to get back to his friends and lover. Almost mad with frustration he watched a huge slow moving car creeping down main street. The female driver appeared to be 200 years old with skin like an alligator, and could only have been looking through the small slice of windshield she could see through the steering wheel.

"She doesn't need any time travel," he muttered to himself, "She probably dated Billy when she was a girl". Martin laughed to himself at the joke and crouched at the ready. He decided he'd throw himself in front of the car, reasoning that her 7mph speed wouldn't kill him, but it might just be enough to send him back in time 140 years, give or take. As the car approach Martin sprinted from the ditch and threw himself across the hood. A great sickening "thud" was heard as he slid off and hit the ground hard. For a moment Martin could see some light, but it faded quickly as the big man dropped into unconsciousness.

34

A tiny ray of light pierced the darkness in Martin's head. As the light became brighter, he was forced to open his eyes, barely remembering what had transpired to put him in such a state. As two pinholes of the day's sunlight pierced his consciousness, he pried open his eyes. The first sight he saw were a pair of ancient leather boots, the kind favored by cowboys and horse thieves of the late 1800's. Before speaking he let out a little groan as his body lay on the hard street. "Uuugggg. I made it. I made it!" he said as he tried to push his body up and get his legs underneath him.

"That was a pretty stupid stunt hombre, you hear?" The man in the boots clearly wasn't impressed and as Martin finally opened his eyes wider, his excitement turned to disappointment as he realized the man in boots was only a tourist and he was exactly in the same year now as he had been 5 minutes ago. The tourist's pinched face and demeaning smile got under Martin's skin. A bright green tee shirt peeked out from a few undone buttons of his dirty reenactors vest. He stood there with a large stack of papers in his hand, holding them as if they were a holy scripture. By this point a small gathering of people had come to Martin's aid and tried to help him to his feet.

"Stop! Don't move him" came the order from someone that appeared to have some EMT training, "he might have broken something."

Martin felt well enough to know he hadn't broken his neck or his back though. "I'm fine, it's just, that car came out of nowhere. People drive like maniacs out here!"

The old woman, who first had been scared by the accident was now mad. Hopping mad. Hearing Martin judge her driving to be maniacal was the last straw.

"Who are you calling a maniac you shit for brains moron?" she taunted him in her creaky old voice, "You jumped in front of me. I'll give you something that'll come out of nowhere Nancy boy!"

With very adept footwork for a lady of her age, she jump stepped in front of the prone Martin and kicked him squarely and solidly in the balls. "*OOOOOOHHHH*!!!" the crowd cried in surprise and sympathy pain as Martin groaned, drooled, and finally passed out from the pain.

PAGE 103

35

For the second time in as many minutes a small tunnel of light permeated Martin brain, waking the man from a pain induced slumber. At first just a pinpoint, it began to expand and demand the big man wake from the kick to the groin that put him under. Martin, aware of the searing pain emanating from his testicles, worked hard to pry his eyes open. After several attempts he got one eye open to see the same old pair of boots staring at him. Both physically and mentally damaged, he let out a groan that said both "I'm in pain" and "Damn, I'm still here" as he waited for the medic to revive him.

"Teebsie! What in the hell are you doing laying here holding your pecker?"

The voice did not come from any modern-day man, and when Martin could again open both eyes he saw a very bemused Doc Scurlock towering over him in the middle of Lincoln's main street.

"I'm back!" Martin said breathlessly, "I made it". While Doc had designs on hacking on Martin for a few more minutes, circumstances decided it would be better to get him off the street. Tensions were running high between Dolan's men and the Regulators after Brady's murder and cartridges could fly at any moment. "C'mon big boy, let's get you off the street." said Doc as he helped the big man to his feet. Still in the throes of pain from Granny Samples' kick to the cojones, Martin hung one arm around Doc's shoulder and used his other hand to hoist his aching balls from bouncing around in his Wranglers.

"Let's git to the store, then we can figure out our next move." said Doc as he dragged Martin toward the portal. Just then Rosita, holding a bucket of eggs she intended to sell, came around the corner. Instinctively her face lit up at seeing her lover, in spite of how their last meeting ended. "*Martin*!" she exclaimed as she saw him limping towards her. As Martin got closer she noticed what she appeared to be a vulgar gesture as he grabbed his manhood, all the while looking in her direction. Filled with rage and disgust at his display she spat on the ground in front of him, "*Puerco*!" she yelled as she turned and stormed off.

Martin, still barely able to breathe sighed heavily. "Don't you worry none Teebsie,

Rosita'll come back as soon as you unhitch your hand from yer balls!" said Doc, laughing way too hard at his own joke.

The two men entered the store, now filled with Regulators who seemed on high alert as they held their Winchesters close and kept their eyes trained across the street toward the saloon.

It was Billy who spoke first, "Hey Teebsie, drop your pecker if you don't mind. Ain't nobody in this store interested!". Chavez, Charlie, and French roared with laughter as Billy's face broke into a wide grin. "Ain't I told you not to come back here no more?" asked Billy, "It took them damn near an hour to scoop up all of Matthews brains. Course, I'da figured that dumb ass didn't have but a teaspoon's worth."

Martin looked seriously at Billy, remembering now that he was a wanted man and would more likely hang than ever return alive to 2020. "Billy, I came back because I've got to talk to you." said Martin carefully. The rest of the Regulators glanced around but none seemed to know what was going on between the two men.

"I can't talk to you looking like some damned clown. Corbett, get this guy some proper clothes if you will." commanded Billy. Sam Corbett, the shopkeeper for Tunstall's store appeared from a back room and motioned for Martin to follow him. Eager to get his talk with Billy over with, Martin sighed and followed him to Tunstall's private rooms. "And Corbett, burn that clown suit he's wearing," Billy added, "If'n he don't hang for killing Matthews, they'll sure as hell hang him for wearing that!" Once again the Regulators broke down in laughter at Martin's expense and the final giggles swirled around the room as he disappeared.

"Damn sure Billy, Dolan's got a lot of new boys over there. Where they all coming from?" asked diminutive Charlie Bowdre. "Hell if I know Charlie" replied Billy, "But most of em probably don't know which end of Sam Colt to hold onto, so I wouldn't worry much if I was you." Bowdre gave a small nod to Billy, although with the group at the saloon swelling to what looked liked thirty or more Dolan men, he wasn't sure he believed the young outlaw.

"Let em come," growled French, "The faster they come, the faster they die". Billy pasted a satisfied smile on his face at the comment as Doc slowly craned his head from the window, "We might could use some reinforcements of our own Billy."

Just then with the clap of boots on a wood floor, Martin Teebs walked back into the room. Dressed in a black frock coat, black trousers, a white bib shirt and deep maroon vest, he looked the very essence of a Lincoln County badman. Martin awkwardly adjusted his hat on head and fidgeted with the Winchester in his left hand. On his right hip he wore a '73 Colt single action Army. Billy beamed at him like a proud younger brother, "Ask and you shall receive Doc. reinforcements have arrived!".

Chavez turned to see Martin' transformation and exclaimed, "Damn Teebsie, you keep dressing like that and Rosita might even come back". Martin smiled an "aw shucks" smile and turned back to Billy. "Billy, can we please talk?" he asked even more cautiously than the first time. Always in good spirits Billy responded, "Sure, what's up Teebsie?". Martin measured the young man, trying to determine if he knew what the conversation was going to be about, or if he was just being his laconic self. "I mean in private, please?" said Martin as he motioned toward Tunstall's room.

Billy looked blankly at his friend, and then around the room at his little band of brothers. "Alright." he said, with as little emotion as he could muster. The two men walked toward the back of the store, and then out of sight of the Regulators, still on guard, and still waiting for Dolan's retribution that would surely be coming.

36

Billy sat down on a light blue stool that he figured the high class Tunstall used when he slipped his boots on each morning. "Alright Teebsie, shoot." he said, staring Martin directly in the eyes.

Martin took a deep breath to gather himself before he spoke, "Billy, when I was here last time, I lost something. Something of mine. Something important, and I know you found it."

"You lost your girl, I saw that, but I ain't found her. Hell, she ain't even really missing." said Billy as he suspiciously raised his eyes at Martin.

"That's not what I'm talking about, and you know it. I lost my book and I want it back!" demanded Martin.

"Book huh? Hey Teebsie, did I ever tell ya that when I was a kid in Silver City I loved to read?" asked Billy. Martin, sensing a stall tactic went right for the jugular "Damnit Billy! That's MY book. You have no right having it. You have no idea what could happen if you…." Martin was lost for words, not knowing how to portray to an 18 year old cattle thief and gunfighter the ramifications of messing with history, and with time itself.

"I sure did love to read. I got that from my Mama I'm sure." said Billy as a slight smile in remembrance of his mother settled on his face.

"Come on Billy, just give me the book. Please!" implored Martin.

Continuing to have a different conversation than the one Martin was having, Billy went on, "She was a fine woman Teebsie. She died though. Man, I was only 14. Galloping consumption. You ever seen someone die of consumption?"

Martin's heart began to race faster and he seemed out of breath as the situation was slipping from his control, "No", he said, "and I'm sorry to hear about your Mom Billy, but you can't have that book!"

"Man Teebsie, it ain't pretty. Coughing up blood day after day. Fever that'll roast yer brain. It was hard to watch. If there was some way I could have known my mama was going to get sick, I'da done everything in my power to stop it, ya know?" Billy looked directly at Martin, "Anything at all my friend. But, how could somebody know something like that before it ever happened….right?" Billy stare taunted Martin to respond. Surely by now the Kid had read the book, or at least glanced over it. He must know Martin was not some bumbling 1870's handyman. He must know that his friend Martin Teebs had somehow come from another time. Could Billy even conceive of time travel? Would he be able to understand the ramifications of messing with history? Was he simply toying with Martin or would he seriously consider keeping (and using) a book that could spin history off of its delicate axis?

Exasperated, Martin appealed with the only bargaining chip he had left. "Look Billy, just give me the book. I'll stay here. I'll fight with you. Hell, I'll even die with you, but I just need to have that book back."

Billy looked past Martin as if searching for some long-lost memory. "I sure did love to do me some reading back in Silver. When this thing is all over, I think I'm gonna sit right down and do me some more Teebsie." With that Billy rose from the stool and clapped Martin on the shoulder, "Looking good hombre. Like a natural born killer. Let's us go on up front and see about all that fighting and dying stuff you was talking about."

Martin, thoroughly defeated, let his eyes gaze upon the floor. The young outlaw walked out of the room, and moments later, his much older friend followed him into history, and possibly into eternity.

37

Billy and Martin reentered the Tunstall store's main room to find it deserted, except for Sam Corbett, who still insisted on getting dressed in his storekeepers clothing every day, even though the store had long since ceased to be open to the public. The last customer through the door was the one seeing John Tunstall's body being brought into town after his murder weeks ago.

Martin and Billy look at each other questioningly and then spied movement on the porch. Seeing the men had taken up posts outside meant either a fight was about to break out, or there was no chance of one. Either way, Billy wanted to be part of the action. "Let's see what them fellers are doing out there Teebsie." drawled the young outlaw. Stepping onto the porch into brilliant sunshine, Billy scanned the street, seeing a growing mob of Dolan's men spilling out of the saloon.

"What's going on Doc?" asked Billy, "You figure they's getting ready to start something?"

"Nah, if they was gonna let loose, they'da done it by now. They're just bellyaching is all." replied the older man.

French took time to purposely load his Winchester in front of Dolan's boys, slowly sliding each round into the carbine while giving them a satisfied look, as if he had a name and face picked out for each bullet. Not to be outdone, several of Dolan's men drew their revolvers, opened the loading gate, and spun the cylinder as if to check if they were fully loaded. Neither side seemed itching for a fight however and both bands of men resembled nothing if not two peacocks preening on the dusty street. Amid the general clicking and occasional insult, Charlie was the first to voice his concern, "Damn Billy, Dolan's sure got a lotta boys these days."

Scanning the horde Billy clucked his tongue in assent "Sure does. I wonder where they're all coming from? Some of them I ain't ever seen around these parts before." Silent until now, Martin took a closer look at the mob of heavily armed men. Exiting the saloon, one man looked conspicuously out of place, hurriedly buttoning his shirt. Before he could finish the job, Martin was shocked to see a bright green tee shirt with the words "New Jersey" emblazoned upon it underneath. Martin' jaw dropped and his eyes went wide, realizing he was not the only inhabitant of the future in Lincoln, NM circa 1878.

"What?" Martin said incredulously, to no one in particular. The man, finally suited for battle, cast a glance across the street to the Tunstall store and locked gazes with Martin. His narrow face pinched up like a snake that might strike. Martin quickly looked away as if to regain his composure. "What's the matter Teebsie?" asked Billy, "You look like you seen a ghost or sumpthin."

Martin nervously looked around trying to distract the Regulators from seeing what he saw. They all slowly turned their head towards him, waiting for him to speak. "Ummm, nothing. It's nothing," Martin replied, "Just feeling queasy, probably from that kick to the nuts." Billy and Doc locked glances, both with the same question in mind. "Kick to the nuts? What in the hell are you talkin bout? Who kicked you in the nuts?"

Martin exhaled mightily, realizing that the kick happened in 2020 and even Doc wouldn't have known it. "You know what guys, forget it. I was joking." Doc shook his head while Chavez and French gave Martin a look that you might to a crazy person, just before they were carted off the asylum.

"I just need some air, that's all," said Martin, "I'm just going to walk around back." With Dolan's men presenting a more pressing threat, Billy decided to let Martin go, focusing his attention on the growing concern across the street. Martin, his new clothes, and his guns walked around the corner of the Tunstall store and out of sight.

38

Martin crunched through the dry grass along Bonito Creek, searching. His mission on this trip back in time was twofold. First, he had to get his book back to keep Billy from using the information in it to change history. Failing miserably at that, he held out hope that his friendship with The Kid might allow him to get close enough to figure out where it was, and then to take the book back to its rightful place in time. Priority two was something completely different. He had to find Rosita. Unless hers was to be an immaculate conception, Martin had to assume that they met at least one more time, since he couldn't remember a time when they had been intimate. More than that, the woman seemed to truly love him, and he also had to assume that he loved her in some strange way. That feeling left him warm and cold at the same time, since he was legally and (mostly) happily married to Lilly. The same Lilly who would surely leave him or have him committed if she knew he was a murderer, adulterer, and time traveler. Martin contemplated these various vocations as he walked in vain toward the east, hoping to come across Rosita or someone that could point him in her direction.

As a murderer, Martin was batting 1000. Hall of fame numbers. One shot, one kill, and a lawman to boot. Of all the things he tried in life, murder seemed to be the thing he was most successful at. He certainly couldn't say the same for his job at the ad agency. He also seemed to have a knack for adultery, at least as far as he could tell. How Martin Teebs, he of the half gallon of ice cream eating fame, could possibly have the most beautiful woman in the territory fall in love with him seemed impossible. But strange as it seemed, the pictures in the Patron House undeniably showed that Rosita did have a baby boy named Martin Jr. and that he was named after the father. So, while Martin and Lilly's romance had long since grown tepid, it appeared that he still had bullets in the gun when the time to shoot came.

When it came to time travel, the real, hapless Martin Teebs appeared. Castigating himself for losing the book, then reasoning that during Brady's assassination it was the book or his life, Martin realized that as a time traveler, he made a pretty good quality control manager at an ad agency.

"Well, 2 out of 3 ain't bad." he murmured to himself as he crunched along the dry grass.

While Lincoln was built along one only main street there were a number of alleyways leading to small huts, stables, and barns all sitting just off of the road. About to give up and afraid of being shot by Dolan's men while out here alone, Martin rounded a corner from behind a barn. On either side of the small strip of dirt, just back from the main road were two adobe huts that had seen many better days. Hearing a door swing open, Martin was shocked and pleased to see the very beautiful Rosita Luna step out, carry a basket of laundry.

"Rosita!" Martin cried as she stepped into the street.

The woman craned her neck to see who had been hiding down near the creek. With his black clothes, guns, and boots Rosita didn't recognize him at first. Martin scurried closer as she tried to match the well-known voice with the new image of the man standing in front of her.

"*Martin*?" she asked cautiously.

Martin ran up to her about to throw his arms around her as she dropped the basket of laundry in the street to stop him.

"Oh Rosita, I found you," Martin breathed heavily, "I'm so glad I found you."

The shock of seeing Martin looking like he actually belonged in Lincoln over, she seethed at the memory of their last meeting. "Who dressed you, your wife?" she nearly spat the words at him.

"I want to explain that Rosita, please?" Martin implored.

Growing angrier, Rosita's voice raised in pitch and volume "Explain!? Go ahead *Martin*, explain!" Rosita waved her hands in Martin's face as if coaxing an answer from him.

Martin fumbled for words "Well, I…"

"Explain how it is you go from here for weeks, no, months at a time *Martin*! Explain how you never tell me where you go or when you'll be back *Martin*! Explain how you expect me each time to take you back, no question asked *Martin*!!" Rosita's voice grew angrier as she delivered the last salvo, "And when you do return you tell me you have a wife! *Esposa*!! Can you explain THAT *Martin*!!??"

Martin stood in the middle of the street, punch drunk from the verbal beating. He wanted nothing more than to melt into Rosita's arms and have everything be ok. Standing there with her breasts heaving, her raven hair blowing lightly in the breeze and her arms crossed in challenge, he knew his chances were running out. Finally, he spoke, "I can't explain everything Rosita, not right now anyway. Believe me, I wish I could." Rosita sneered at him and raised her chin defiantly. "But," he continued, "I do know we belong together. I've seen it. I'm sure of it."

"I wouldn't be so sure of that *pobrecito.*" was her reply, dripping with sarcasm.

Martin took a chance and reached out to grab her hand as he spoke "It's true Rosita, I belong to you, and you? You belong to me."

Rosita's internal fortress crumbled as Martin's words unlocked the feelings she'd been guarding for him. She crumpled into his arms, sobbing wildly, "Oh *mi amor*! Please, please don't leave me again!" Martin held her tightly knowing it was a promise he couldn't make. Not now anyway. "I can't promise that now Rosita. There are men after me. I can't risk them hurting you. I couldn't live with that. I promise I will come back. No matter what it takes….I'll be back."

Rosita buried her face into Martin's chest. She felt so small and slight in his arms, as if a stiff wind might blow her away. He reached down and raised her chin and they kissed. Lightly at first, and then more deeply. Her eyes shining through her tears, she said, "You promise? *Si?*"

With a slight nod of his head and a smile spreading across his face he simply mouthed the word "yes" back at her. Rosita wiped the tears from her eyes and whisked the hair from her face. Suddenly in control again, she smiled strongly at Martin, "Come *mi amor*, you must be hungry. I shall cook for you."

For a moment Martin felt the most whole, the most complete that he'd ever felt in his life and smiled back at the woman he must surely love. Only a commotion from behind them on the main street snapped the two lovers from their spell. Coming towards them were a number of the Dolan gang, led by newly minted Sheriff George Peppin. They were very obviously very drunk, and probably dangerous. The thought crossed Martin's mind that he was good at 2 of 3 things and killing was one of them. He wondered if he was going to have to use his newfound skill again sooner than expected?

39

Dolan's men sat around the saloon bitching and complaining. With Brady dead, George "Dad" Peppin had been appointed Sheriff of Lincoln County. Peppin hadn't shown much disposition to go after The Regulators, as Tunstall's hired thugs had come to call themselves, and his men were growing antsy. Beaver Smith was not long for the troubled streets of Lincoln, having just secured a new building in the tiny hamlet of Fort Sumner, but on this day he did his best to sling as much whiskey as the boys would drink, hoping it would keep a fight from breaking out and draining the till in repairs, broken bottles, and the cleaning up of blood.

"Smith!" growled a narrow-faced man, "More whiskey…for all of em. I want to make a toast". The man waved his hand across the crowd for emphasis as Smith complied with the order. First sitting, and then standing on a barstool, the man, whom no one seemed to know or remember barked at the top of his lungs. "Here's to that prissy Englishman Tunstall! May he rest in misery!" The men's heads shot around at the mention of Tunstall, and a few began to cheer.

"Cast him to history and cast him to hell!" the man continued as Dolan's mob began to support the message being delivered by the mysterious orator.

Peppin stepped gingerly up to the bar to grab another shot, sitting down near the door. His look at the stranger conveyed confusion and amusement at the same time.

"You know what I call one dead Englishman?" the stranger roared.

"What?" came the resounding reply from all in attendance.

"A pretty good start!!" shouted the man as Dolan's group exploded in cheers and laughter.

"Come boys, these streets belong to us! Let us show those damned Regulators what a bunch of real men look like!" concluded the man as he hopped off the stool and walked toward the exit.

"Howdy stranger," said Peppin as the man approached him, "I don't think I've ever seen you round these parts. Where is it you come from?"

Carl Farber smiled knowingly at the Sheriff and clapped him on the shoulder as he replied matter of factly, "Friend, you wouldn't believe me if I told you."

40

The noisy gaggle of drunken men approached Rosita's home as Martin eyed them, deciding on his next move. "Come on Rosita, let's go inside" he said, gathering up the laundry basket, "they're just drunk". Rosita walked toward the door as Martin shuffled backwards never taking his eyes off the mob. Suddenly one of them shouted out, "There he is! He killed Matthews…son of a bitch!" Martin pressed back further with his Winchester at the ready. "Blew his damn brains out!" shouted another.

Rosita quickly walked inside the house and tugged Martin's arm to come with her. "You gonna let your girl fight for you yella!!" screamed a voice from the back of the crowd.

"*Martin*! Please, come in now!" cried Rosita tugging harder on Martin's arm, "Please!!". Martin took one step back and caught his bootheel on the threshold. Along with Rosita's pulling he fell back and hit his head hard on the adobe wall. Pitching forward to his knees he heard Rosita screaming his name as his Winchester fell in the dirt and his vision went black.

Dolan's men, too drunk to even understand what happened ambled around for a bit and began to walk off. One or two of them fell over in a drunken stupor. As the drunken crowd dissipated, a small, grizzled man in the back of the group yelled out "Not much Mary Ann!" Only one narrow faced man walked closer and closer to Rosita's house, intrigued with her and the man she had been seen with. Her eyes filled with tears, and wide with fear, Rosita quickly grabbed the Winchester from where Martin had been only a moment before. She backed inside her home and barred the door closed.

Carl Farber stopped in his tracks, not wanting to risk getting shot. As he turned back to Dolan's men, he saw only Peppin still standing there, incredulous at what he's just seen. "You see that?" Farber inquired of the Sheriff. Peppin looked confused, maybe even a little scared. "What the hell?" he mused as he stared at the patch of dirt where Martin Teebs used to be, just seconds ago.

"You asked where I'm from?" said Farber through a crooked grin. "I'm from where he's from" he said with a satisfying smile while pointing with his thumb to a now vacant spot that was formerly occupied by Martin Henry Teebs.

41

A searing pain shot thru Martin's head as a red light started to cut through the blackness. He threw his arms out in front of him and shouted, "Rosita! Rosita!". As his vision slowly returned he scrambled wildly around for his guns, none of which could be found. In a panic he jumped to his feet, still barely able to see. Expecting to be attacked by Dolan's rowdies at any minute, he instead heard children's laughter behind him. He whirled around to see two very modern looking boys playing with a very modern soccer ball. "No!" he sniffed, "No, no, no!!"

Realizing the knock on the head had taken him back to modern day, Martin felt the pit of his stomach dropping. "Oh Rosita." he said through gasping breaths.

Tourists walked by the big man who seemed to have been crying. They imagined in his 1878 era clothes he was probably a living history reenactor and was putting on some sort of show. A few pointed, one or two laughed, and a group of Japanese tourists, all wearing surgical masks, took his picture. Just across the road Lilly peered out onto the street from the main Patron house seeing her husband flailing about, the object of unwanted tourist attention. She slowly put her bra back on and began to button her blouse as she quietly shook her head. Just behind her a shadowy figure with great abs scurried out of the room.

42

The cool air streaming from the overhead vent was in stark contrast to the dry desert air the Teebs had just spent almost a week in. Martin sat stiffly in his too small coach seat, staring ahead, replaying the events of past and present in his head. "Well, that was," Lilly paused to find the right word "interesting. Wasn't it Martin?"

Martin, lost in his own thoughts, failed to respond. More than in his real, modern life, in his past that he presumed was actually real, he was a failure. He'd failed to recover his book from Billy, he'd murdered a legally appointed officer of the law, and in his most spectacular failure, he hadn't been able to impregnate Rosita as history demanded. He wondered, was history already changed? Would little Martin Jr. cease to exist? After his breakdown on the main street, he hadn't the forethought to look at Rosita's picture in the main Patron house to see if Junior was still there. Martin imagined a "Back to Future" scene where the baby's picture would slowly fade out as Martin failed to sire him. Martin wondered, was failing to create Martin Jr, and thereby erasing his life, worse than ending Billy Matthews'? Was Martin guilty of sending 2 people to the great unknown, one of them before he was ever born?

And what of Billy? Certainly, with the information in Bachaca's book he could turn the tide of the Lincoln County War. In fact, Billy could change the outcomes of just about everyone in Lincoln County if he wanted to. Martin was vaguely aware of a concept called The Butterfly Effect that posited a gentle flapping of a butterfly's wings in China would eventually disturb the air halfway around the world. If Billy made even one small change in the timeline of history, the results could be disastrous. Could Billy be blamed? At present, Martin was relying on the impulses of a late teens young man to use the information in the book responsibly. Teebs even wondered to himself, what if he found next week's newspaper? Would he be tempted to buy the winning Lotto ticket? Would he lay bets on all the winning sports teams? Would he predict major world events happening just a few days away? Even at his more mature age, Martin couldn't be sure he wouldn't use that knowledge for his own personal gain, so how did he expect Billy to?

Time and again though, Martin's thoughts turned to Rosita. How such a beautiful woman, full of life, could somehow pick him mystified Martin. They must have met before in some fold in time, as Rosita clearly knew him the first time he traveled back in time to 1878 Lincoln. In fact, everybody knew Martin so he surmised that he had a much longer history in New Mexico than just two visits. If so, he wondered, why wasn't a Martin Teebs in the history books? All the familiar names were in every single book he'd purchased about The Kid and the Lincoln County War. Scurlock, Folliard, French, Bowdrie. Bonney, and more. But no Martin Teebs…not even once. Unable to solve the puzzle at the moment, Martin was at least warmed by the fact that he was sure, somehow, to have another visit to his new friends and love. There had to be some other point in time he was to be inserted into in order to meet and befriend Billy, and to win Rosita's heart. Not knowing how or when this time travel thing might happen again, Martin focused on the day when he'd be transported back to the glory days of 1878 and to the life he never knew that he loved, until now.

He closed his eyes and let the cool air shower his forehead. In the twilight moments just before nodding off, he felt Rosita's hand slide under his. With a jolt his eyes shot wide open, and he turned his head expectantly to his right, only to see the hand belonged not to Rosita, but to his wife Lilly. His wife, he reminded himself firmly, the woman he married many years ago, for better…or for worse.

"I'm sorry hun. Did I wake you?" Lilly asked.

Martin shook the century old cobwebs from his brain before replying, "No, no. I was just thinking of our trip. How nice of a time we had."

Lilly smiled a tight little smile, "Yes, it was fun. Now back to the real world."

Martin's sad smile caught Lilly by surprise, so she let his hand go and picked up a magazine. Martin turned his head back to the cool air and allowed his mind to drift back to a time when he was something else. A real man, a lover, a father, a Regulator.

43

Colin rushed into Martin's cubicle with a start. "Marty!" he exclaimed, "what are you doing?". At that very moment, Martin was thinking about his past in Lincoln, just as he did most every waking moment in the two weeks since he and Lilly had returned. What he wasn't doing was any meaningful work, which also was a byproduct of his trip to the deserts of New Mexico. He had taken to poring over his library of Billy the Kid books, hoping that somehow his name would appear in one of them and explain his strange journey. He hoped, beyond hope, that he might even learn of his first meeting with Billy and Rosita, so he could appropriately prepare for it. So far his efforts had been fruitless, and on this morning he was flipping through a few more pages, vainly searching for the name of the great Regulator Martin Teebs. His fingers quickly slammed Bachaca's book closed (Martin had purchased another copy just days ago). "Umm, just working. What's up Colin?" said Martin in a voice he wished had more enthusiasm. Colin eyed the now familiar Billy the Kid book suspiciously but decided it wasn't worth asking Martin what exactly he was "working" on.

"Hey, I'm applying for the new sales job. Did you see it? What do you think?" gushed Colin.

"Sales job?" said Martin, "Don't know anything about it. Are you sure *you* want to be in sales Colin?"

Colin looked slightly wounded by the question so much so that Martin jumped back in, "I mean, you've never done it. How do you know you'll like it?"

"I don't," said the younger man, "but if I want to move up and move out, this is the route to take me there. What about you Marty, are you going to apply?"

Martin pondered the question. He'd spent 17 years in exactly the same job he was in right now. In the same cubicle in fact. While he had visions of grandeur when he was younger, now he just wanted to get a paycheck, go home, and dream about being a Regulator. "I don't think so Colin, I kind of like my job. Besides, I'll bet it's a lot of driving and sitting in traffic in the city."

Colin shrugged his shoulders with a grin, "Okay then. And yeah, I'll bet there's tons of traffic in LA." The mention of Los Angeles caught Martin off guard, "LA? What do you mean? How's that happening?"

Colin was already dancing, lighter than air back to his cubicle as the muttered over his shoulder, "We're opening a new west coast office. Don't you read your email?"

Martin sat for a moment, wondering how something so big had slipped past his radar. If he was being truthful, he knew that he'd barely paid attention to his work over the past 2 weeks. It must have been announced while he was in New Mexico or shortly after he returned. Curiosity getting the better of him, he began to search his inbox and found the email hiding just below a survey the airline had sent him asking how his return flight was. Clicking on the emailed titled "New West Coast Expansion" brought Martin to what seemed like an internal job posting. As he scoured it to see what important info he'd missed, his heart stopped beating momentarily and his breath became rapid and shallow. Just under the announcement the posting read:

West Coast Sales Territory – Extensive travel to California, Nevada, Utah, Colorado, Arizona, and New Mexico.

Martin eyes were transfixed by the tiny blinking cursor next to the words New Mexico. He'd spent the better part of his post Lincoln time figuring out how he'd ever get back to set things right with Rosita and to retrieve his book. Now, here, right before his eyes was the answer. A sales trip that included New Mexico even once would allow him to fix the past, and maybe his future. If the job demanded monthly trips, well….Martin could only imagine the possibilities.

"Sales huh?" he mused. While Martin had never sold a thing in his life, he'd gotten pretty good at negotiating for the players he wanted on his fantasy football team. If he could talk Colin out of drafting Patrick Mahomes, he must have some powers of persuasion, he reasoned.

"Colin." Martin muttered. What if he applied for the job and got it over his young friend? Colin seemed so excited by the prospect of a new job that Martin couldn't bear to take it away from him. Colin had asked him if he was going to apply however, so he must have at least entertained the thought that the two friends might compete for one job. Martin looked out into the bullpen and saw Colin's head bobbing up and down, clearly excitedly talking to someone…probably about his upcoming interview. Realizing he had no better prospects to ever get back to New Mexico, Martin quickly typed out an email to the Human Resources manager expressing his interest in the job and his confidence that he could be the best darn salesperson the company had ever seen. With a final glance at Colin he hit the send key, opened Bachaca's book and sighed with exhaustion having just done more work in 5 minutes then he'd done in the past two weeks.

44

"Lil! Lil!" yelled Martin as he stampeded through the front door. With eyes alight and a menacing smile on his face Martin could have been delivering good news, or reenacting a famous scene from the movie The Shining.

Talking to someone on the phone Lilly saw the look of excitement on her husband's face. "Faith, let me go. Martin's home and he looks like he wants to talk. Yeah, I'll call you next week. Bye hon." said Lilly as she gently replaced the phone. "Ok big boy, where's the fire?" she said in good humor.

"Lil, you're not going to believe what I did!" gushed Martin unable to control himself, "My company is opening a new office and they need a new salesperson. I applied for the job!"

If a regular sized feather had a tiny baby feather and you cut that in half, it would still have been enough to knock Lilly Teebs over and place her flat on the ground. In 17 years, not once did Martin ever express any interest in climbing the corporate ladder. She practically had to twist his arm to go and ask for his annual cost of living raise. To her, he seemed to be happily mired in mediocrity, and would never change. The news, to say the least, was stunning.

"Sales, Martin," she questioned, "is that really what you want to do?"

Martin's face took on a look of hurt and Lilly realized that she wasn't exactly being encouraging. "I mean, sales. Yeah. I could see that. Wow, to say I'm proud of you would be an understatement!" said Lilly.

"Thanks Lil. I figured it's time to seek some other opportunities, and this sales thing could be a great fit." Martin confidently replied.

With images of more money, trips to exotic places not named New Mexico, and maybe a new car in her head, Lilly started to catch the same fever that engulfed her husband. "So, where will you be selling? In the city? Newark? Probably Connecticut too?" she asked.

Martin paused for a moment to get up his nerve before stating matter of factly, "We're opening a new office in LA. I would be the west coast sales rep."

"California Martin!" snapped Lilly, "what were you thinking?? We live in New Jersey!"

Martin knew he was on dangerous ground. He loved his wife and didn't want to lie to her. Before speaking he estimated just how much he could bend the truth without it breaking. "Oh, well most of these sales are probably over the phone or internet or something," he lied, "I probably won't have to travel all that much anyway Lil…and besides, I don't have the job yet."

A small bit of concern washed away from Lilly's face at the news. Seeing this, Martin felt like he'd dodged a major bullet and reasoned with himself that he really didn't know what the job entailed just yet. "Ok." said Lilly, "and besides, you don't even have the job yet. So let's just see what happens."

Despite his wife's concerns, Martin's good feelings had already returned as he danced his way towards the stairs. "That's the magic word Lil, yet!" he exclaimed as he headed upstairs to dress down for dinner.

45

"Soooo Martin, you've been with us for, what, 17 years?" said Randall Talbot, "And all in the same job." Talbot was tasked with interviewing candidates for the new office in Los Angeles and seemed perplexed by the man sitting across the desk from him. "That's rather unusual," he said and paused before adding, "we don't generally have anyone who stays in the same job for more than a few years."

Sensing he might be failing the interview before it even got started, Martin reached for anything that would explain his near permanence in cubicle #31 over the past 17 years. "Well Sir," he began "I love this company. In all the years I've been here, I just haven't found anything else that really fits me." Martin quickly added, "Until this sales job of course!"

Talbot looked warily at the big man trying to figure out what possibly motivated him to apply for a job on the other side of the country? "You know Martin, this job requires a lot of travel. LA, Sacramento, Denver, Phoenix. It might even involve relocation at some point. Are you sure you're up for all of that?" Somewhere in the back of Martin's mind the wind blew a cloud of dust down Lincoln's main street. Through the dust strode Rosita, breasts heaving, hips swaying, biting her lip in hunger for the man she loved. In his mind, he strode gallantly up to her, scooping her into his arms, and taking her to the bed where he would make love to her as no man had ever before. Her soft, breathy moans would paint a symphony of desire that neither of them could escape. Upon completion, Rosita's orgasmic smile would let Martin know that he'd fulfilled his commitment to history, and that the very beginnings of his boy, Martin Jr., were already taking shape. He breathed heavily into the dream, feeling more satiated than he had in a very long time.

"Martin!" exclaimed Talbot shaking Martin from his daydream "did you hear what I said?"

"Oh, yes sir. Sorry sir." Martin was embarrassed, but at least glad that Talbot wasn't able to read his thoughts. "Sir, I love the west. I've been there sir. In fact, in a way I'm still there. Do you know what I mean Mr. Talbot?"

Talbot hadn't the slightest idea what Martin Teebs was talking about and didn't pretend to. He looked over the rim of his glasses at Martin and wondered if the big man could even sell ice water to a man dying of thirst. He asked a few more perfunctory questions that Martin gave very predictable answers to. Talbot had enough information to go on, so he moved to end the interview as quickly as possible.

"Thanks for coming in Martin," said Talbot quickly rising and shoving his hand toward Martin, "We'll let you know."

Martin took the hint and after a much too enthusiastic handshake, he started for the door. At the last moment some inner fire prompted him to turn around and state "I'm ready. I'm ready for this job, and to make this company a LOT of money Sir!" To emphasize his point Martin threw both thumbs in the air and cocked his head while smiling at Talbot. Talbot, lost on how to respond, reluctantly raised a single thumb and gave Martin a rueful smile. With a shake of his head and a wave of his hand, he dismissed the big man.

"Well, that went pretty good." Martin thought to himself. As he settled into cubicle #31 he saw Colin bounding his way.

"Well, how'd it go? Did you get the job Marty?" asked Colin.

Martin, still in the throes of post interview analysis said "Well, no. I mean, not yet. They still have interviews to do."

Forcing the issue, Colin replied "Yeah, but you're gonna get it, right? You think so?"

"Easy now Colin. There's some tough competition, including you." offered Martin.

"Oh no, I pulled my hat out of the ring Marty. I'm not interviewing for the job anymore." said Colin.

Martin was surprised. He only learned about the job because of Colin's excitement in applying for it. "Wait. What? Why?"

Colin shrugged and exhaled loudly "Have you ever been in sales Marty?" Martin carefully shook his head no. "It's all about the numbers," continued Colin, "all day, every day, numbers, quota, dollars, sales, numbers. It's relentless. They never let up."

"Ok!" snapped Martin, "I get it. The numbers count. I get it." Martin was worried he came on too strong but Colin didn't seem to notice.

"Anyway Marty, good luck. I hope you get it. I know you'll do great!" gushed Colin leaving Martin feeling more than a little guilty.

Martin could only offer a weak smile as Colin shuffled back to his cubicle. What if he DID get the job? How would he reach those numbers month after month after month? Remembering Talbot's strange look when he left, Martin was momentarily comforted by the fact that he was fairly certain he wouldn't be offered the job anyway.

But, what if he was?

46

One week later Martin made his way out to his very sensible car, ready for another forgettable day at the office. As he slowly backed into the street another car came screaming towards him, its occupant clearly late for whatever meaningful work they did for a living. At the last moment Martin saw the car and jammed his brakes on exclaiming loudly to no one "What the hell man!!?" The driver, indeed a man, slowed and scowled with his pinched little face as Martin's blood ran cold. It was the guy from Lincoln. The other time traveler, Dolan's man, he was sure of it.

The man reached over to manually roll down the non-power windows on his aged sedan and sneered at Martin "What's your problem baby wipe?" Temporarily silenced by what he thought might be an insult, he finally regained his composure and responded "What's *your* problem? It's 25 miles an hour here!". The man laughed a derisive laugh and attempted to spit out the window at Martin, but the product only made it as far as the door sash, splashing down the side of his car. Shaking his head in disgust, Martin spoke again "Get out of the way, I've got to get to work!".

With that, the man revved his engine and took off like a rocket down the street. Not to be outdone, Martin floored it and took off after him. Both cars flew at well above the speed limit as they approached a school zone. With the bright yellow 15MPH sign blinking the race continued, albeit at a much slower pace. Pulling up next to his rival Martin yelled "What the hell is your problem?" to which the man quickly responded "I've got no problems shortcake, but you have one big one…me!" Martin was tempted to kick the cruise control up to 16mph but the thought of a speeding ticket in a school zone, and rising insurance costs kept him in check. Both men wove their cars back and forth as if warming their tires for the start of a NASCAR race. Just as they exited the school zone they came upon a red light. The men, rivals now in present *and* past faced each other, neither seeming to want to talk about the very obvious elephant in the historical room.

"Listen, just stay the hell away from my.." Martin paused as he wasn't sure what to call the Regulators and Rosita, "..friends if you know what's good for you!"

"Friends? Ha! That's rich. Those worthless losers found the right guy when they took up with you." sneered Farber.

Incensed at the insult to his newly found friends, Martin revved his engine in anger. Farber responded in kind with the distinct clicking of the valves as is likely to happen to a 20-year-old sedan with over 200K miles on it.

"Best thing you can do twinkie" said Farber "is to stay away from me. Because I…I am your worst nightmare."

Martin looked over the faded paint on Farber's car, the spittle dripping down the passenger door, the sure to be Member's Only jacket he was wearing, and the pilling on his way too worn-out khakis and muttered "Well, I can't argue with that"

Just then the light turned green, and Farber nailed the accelerator making a quick left turn away from Martin. In his haste and anger Martin also stomped on the pedal, running right into the rear bumper of the chief of police of Waldwick, NJ.

47

"Lil! Lil! I did it Lil! I got the Job!" yelled Martin as he bounded through the door one night just a week later. Not getting the response he expected, or any response for that matter, he rushed into the kitchen, which was lit up as if Lilly might be nearby. "Lil? Lil?" asked Martin but the quiet house offered no clues to where his wife might be. Deciding she must be upstairs Martin trotted up the staircase and almost strode right by the extra bedroom, dimly lit only by the light of Lilly's laptop screen.

"Lil! I got the job!" said Martin breathlessly as he came to a screeching halt.

Lilly, lost in whatever she was doing on the computer, seemed shocked by Martin's sudden appearance and slammed the laptop screen down quickly as she composed herself, "What? What did you say Martin?"

"Lil, I got the job. The sales job! I'm the new west coast account manager." Martin's excited tone told Lilly she needed to completely snap back to reality so as to show some support for her husband.

"Really," she asked, "you really got it?" Lilly's tone was a bit too incredulous and it registered on Martin's face. Just as he was about to speak his disappointment she quickly cut back in "I mean, of course you did! Wow, that's incredible Martin. I'm so proud of you!" Lilly silently mouthed the word "wow" again for her own benefit. Had this happened 10-12 years ago, it would have been a welcome reprieve from the middle class trap they'd fallen into. As it was now, it was just a shocker that Martin got off his well-worn office chair and actually showed some initiative.

Martin, confidence restored, smiled a very happy and satisfied smile. "Yep," he said, "I leave for training next week. A whole week in the LA office." He then remembered that Lilly had warned him about the amount of travel the job would require, so he felt it important to add "That's ok, isn't it Lil?"

Reasoning with recent and pressing developments on other fronts in her life, it might not be so bad for Martin to be out of the house for a week she enthusiastically replied "Sure! I mean, if you're going to be this big salesman, you need the training. I'll be fine here hun."

"Super. I'm going to get changed and hey…how about this? Martin Teebs, salesman extraordinaire, will make dinner for YOU tonight!" offered Martin as condolence that Lilly would be all alone and probably desperately lonely for the following week.

Lilly smiled and gave him two thumbs up as Martin scooted out of the room. Processing the turn of events her life had just taken, she lifted the laptop screen and looked at the blinking chat box. The message, from someone called LINCOLNCOUNTYDALLAS6969 read simply "What happened? Where did you go?"

Lilly carefully typed her reply "You're NOT going to believe what he just did".

LINCOLNCOUNTYDALLAS6969 replied simply, "Tell me when I get up there. My flight arrives on Monday. My audition is Tuesday morning" and then added a bunch of silly excited face emojis. Lilly halfway smiled and felt a mixture of fear, excitement, and revulsion of what she was about to do…again.

48

After dinner, Martin sat quietly in his bedroom with laptop and credit card at the ready. He was responsible for making his own travel reservations for his sales training the following week. He felt a twinge of guilt in telling Lilly it was for a week, as his boss, Mr. Talbot was clear it was only 3 days. Martin's plan was to fly to LA on Sunday night, attend the training until Wednesday, and then secretly fly to Albuquerque on Wednesday night. After getting a solid night of sleep he'd wake up early and drive to Lincoln bright and early Thursday morning. Talbot had gladly granted Martin 2 days of personal leave against the 127 or so he had accrued over the years when he and Lilly could either not afford to take a vacation, or couldn't agree on one.

The plan, as it were, was to spend the rest of the week and Saturday in Lincoln. While Martin had no idea if he'd be able to slip back in time, he knew he must try. At the very least he had to get his book back but more importantly he had to see Rosita again. Her image delighted his daydreams and tortured his sleep. No matter the risk, his growing infatuation with the young woman drove him to find her. The picture proved that she had a baby, Martin Jr. At some point their relationship must be consummated, he reasoned. If Martin was being totally honest with himself, he missed Billy and the boys too. While stepping into the hotbed of Lincoln County in 1878, fresh on the heels of his killing of Billy Matthews didn't sound like the most sane idea, he also had people he could rely upon to keep him safe. He had his friend. He had Billy. Martin figured 3 days wasn't much, but it was all he could spare. He'd call Lilly on Saturday morning and tell her his flight had been cancelled so he'd just catch a flight home on Sunday morning….a perfect plan.

"Perfect plan" Martin muttered to himself as his finger hovered over the cheery "Book It!" button, "perfect murderer, adulterer, and liar is more like it." As disgusted as Martin was with himself, he felt that he had started a chain reaction that he was no longer in control of. Rosita *wanted* him and it had been far too long since he felt that from Lilly. Billy and the Regulators seemed to really need him, and no one except perhaps Colin seemed to need him for anything nowadays. In Lincoln, New Mexico 1878 Martin was in demand. In Waldwick, New Jersey 2020, Martin was virtually unknown. He wondered, did he really start this strange trip, or was it preordained? Did Martin actually exist in 1878, or some time thereabouts, or did he just travel back for a few stolen moments. The thought that he somehow crossed the bounds of consciousness from a past life to present was too much for him to fathom. If there was a higher power, he wondered, why was it picking on him? Weren't there more worthy people who could go back in time and kill Hitler, or stop Columbus's atrocities against the Native Americans? How did he, Martin Teebs, get selected to move to the head of the time travel class? Martin's answer was simple…he simply had no idea. "Time to get on with it." he mumbled to himself. With thoughts of his woman and his friends spinning in his head Martin punched the "return" key on his new laptop and nodded his head with certainty that he'd done the right thing. He carefully closed the screen on the laptop and slid it into his briefcase. If he hurried, he could probably convince Lilly to warm him a slice of apple pie with a generous scoop of vanilla ice cream on top.

49

The tires on Martin's tiny rental car crunched loudly on the gravel driveway at Juan Patron's House Bed & Breakfast. Martin had waited until he was out of town to reserve a room, hoping it wouldn't be sold out. He didn't want Dallas or Darlene calling his house in New Jersey to confirm a reservation and having Lilly discover his plan. As the car slowed to a halt he gratefully stepped out of the door and stretched mightily. He'd woken early and was on the road by 6am to avoid the infamous Albuquerque traffic, which was generally one person driving 40 mph in the left lane while looking up to the sky for hot air balloons, while 75 people raced bumper to bumper behind them screaming, cursing, and guns waving as the golden sun peeked over the Sandia Mountains.

After 3 hours nonstop on the road, Martin was glad to finally be back in his home away from home. Hearing the arrival, Darlene Jones came walking down the steps with a big smile and open arms. "Martin!" she exclaimed pulling the big man into her ample bosom "So very good to see you again." Under any other circumstance Martin would have questioned whether the woman was hitting on him, but seeing as he only had eyes only for Rosita, the thought never even occurred.

"Great seeing you too Darlene!" he said, "Where's Dallas?"

"Next to Forth Worth silly!" she replied, having been set up for that joke at least 1000 times a year. "No," she added, "he's back now from some audition he had in New York on Monday. He'll be around before too long."

The boomerang effect of the two men wasn't lost on Martin. While he flung from east coast to west this week, his inertia must have swung Dallas in the other direction. If Martin suspected anything else about Dallas and the other reason for his trip back east, he certainly didn't show it.

"Martin, you're early." said Darlene warmly, "I wasn't expecting you until around lunch. The people in the casita decided to stay an extra night so I'm going to need some time to clean it up once they are out. Why don't you come inside for some breakfast?"

Looking around, Martin breathed in the fresh mountain air. His pulse was starting to race and he couldn't even imagine spending a moment more in the present than he had to. "You know, I've been wanting to research a few more areas of town that I didn't get to last time. I think I'll just head out and look around now."

"Suit yourself big boy! See you in a bit." said Darlene as she scuttled back up the steps. Martin opened the trunk and carefully unpacked the clothes that Billy and Corbett had given him on his last trip. Since his room wasn't ready, Martin looked for a place to change. If he did find the portal to get back to 1878, he wanted to look the part rather than take the near constant ribbing of Billy and boys over his current clothes.

Martin walked down the quiet main street. Thursday morning in Lincoln, NM circa 2020 wasn't exactly prime time. He saw a shopkeeper or two arranging their wares, but otherwise the town was quiet. He approached the Torreon' with hopes that the door would be open so he could slip inside and change clothes, but was greeted with a padlock and a "Do Not Enter" sign. Finally, Martin decided to just walk off into the trees near Bonito Creek and do the deed. Stripping down to his underwear he felt what seemed to be a cold breeze blowing across his chest. Disoriented he grabbed the tree only to look up and see a young Mexican girl in a brightly colored dress staring at him. Caught literally with his pants down Martin attempted a non-threatening smile which of course clearly threatened the girl. She let out a shrill scream and ran toward the road as Martin quickly pulled on his wool pants along with shirt and vest, and tossed his hat on for good measure. As he hurried away from the spot where the girl would surely bring an incensed father Martin realized that the cool breeze had blown him all the way back to 1878, in almost the blink of an eye. The dust covered main street was mostly quiet, but unmistakably not designed for tractor trailers.

He was back in Lincoln…he had arrived.

50

Without weapons, and not knowing what had transpired since his last departure, Martin thought it prudent to stay mostly out of sight. He moved from building to building, carefully on the lookout for any Dolan men. While the town was clearly alive, there didn't seem to be any inkling of the raging Lincoln County War. In fact, it almost seemed downright peaceful. Thinking his services as a Regulator weren't currently needed, Martin made his way to Rosita's small house.

Climbing the 2 steps to the wooden porch Martin slowly knocked on the turquoise blue door, nearly breathless at the prospect of seeing Lincoln's most beautiful woman. Martin closed his eyes at the thought and when he opened them, he was greeted by the cold barrel of a Winchester protruding from the door, pointed alarmingly at his face.

"Hey! Hey, don't shoot!" he yelled. In a flash the barrel disappeared, and the door swung open, Rosita Luna jumping into her lover's arms and burying her face in his chest. "*Martin! Martin!* You are back *mi amor!*" gushed Rosita, her excitement at seeing Martin seemingly even greater than his at seeing her. Their lips, once separated by over a century, now separated by mere inches met hungrily as they kissed deeply. Martin swung her around on the porch before gently placing her down and guiding her inside.

"Where have you been *Martin*? I have missed you so, so much my love." asked Rosita. Unsure of how to answer with any sort of believability, Martin simply replied "I told you I would be back. I told you we belong together." Rosita sighed the way only a woman in love can as she beamed at the big man.

"What's with the rifle answering the door by the way?" Martin wanted to know.

"Oh, I thought you were that Farter, or Farber or whatever that *bastardo's* name is. He came by here looking for you. Telling me you are not coming back. Telling me you are married and that I should find a real man." said Rosita. Martin was incensed at the thought of anyone even coming near Rosita, and he reasoned that Farber must be the name of his drag race rival as well as the New Jersey tee shirt wearing member of Dolan's mob.

PAGE 143

"Did he hurt you?" Martin demanded, wringing his hands as if on Farber's neck.

"No *Martin. Billito* was in town and chased him. I think that little Farter might have wet his pants a little!" laughed Rosita. Martin calmed slightly knowing that his friend Billy would watch over his woman when he wasn't there. "*His friend Billy the Kid*", Martin thought. How in the hell did that happen? Even in his wildest dreams he never imagined any of this…whatever this was.

"Say, where is Billy? I haven't seen any of the guys out there." asked Martin.

Almost as if on cue, there was a sharp rap on the windowpane, startling Martin. He looked out to see Billy and Doc on horseback waving for him to come out. Martin pushed open the window. "Hey, button up loverboy!" laughed Billy as Doc looked on with a smile.

"Hey guys, good to see you. What's up?" asked the big man.

"We got some important decisions to make Teebs" said Doc, "we need to ride out for Patricio. C'mon…and bring your guns."

Martin looked over at Rosita whose concern was genuine and written all over her face. She clasped her hands firmly but said nothing. Martin breathed in heavily the way you do when you're about to do something you've got to do…but probably shouldn't. "Alright guys, gimme just a minute to get ready." he said.

"Hey Teebsie!" shouted Billy "Don't worry none bout Rosita, we got someone watching over her. She'll be jest fine my friend."

Martin put his hat on, strapped on his gun belt, and walked over to Rosita who appeared to be on the verge of tears. "It'll be alright." he said as he kissed her gently. She reached her fingers up to stroke his face, knowing she could not keep him. "Go, do this thing, *si*?" she said, "Then come back to me."

Martin picked up his Winchester and walked out the door where Doc held the reigns to a horse already saddled for him. Not even knowing how he knew how to ride, Martin slung his leg over the saddle and the three men spurred their mounts to the east, out of Lincoln heading for San Patricio…and for their destiny.

51

That evening, the Regulators, some of whom Martin had never met (although they seemed to know him) sat around a campfire in the hills above Patricio. With them was a slim man with a large oriental mustache and a starched white shirt that seemed well out of place in the current environs. Martin quickly came to realize this was Alexander McSween, a partner of Tunstall's and the heir apparent to his small but violent army. The men talked back and forth, with some small arguments breaking out from time to time, until Doc called the men to order.

"Listen up!" he said, "We've been chased outta Lincoln. Dolan and his boys ride the street without a care in the world. They'll tell anyone who'll listen we're yellow. Alex is living up here like some kind of rat, and they're setting up shop in John's store right now!"

The men howled in disapproval at the thought of Jimmy Dolan profiting in any way from the murder of their boss John Tunstall.

While McSween was the de facto leader of the ragtag group of men, he was ill suited for the job. He hated violence and never carried a gun. McSween preferred to use the courts and the law to solve his problems, but recent events had shown him that a paper warrant was woefully inadequate at stopping bullets. He had fled Lincoln knowing that Dolan and his men were coming to finish him off, so as to have all of the economy of Lincoln for themselves once again. His wife Susan was squirreled away safely in a home in San Patricio but even there, McSween feared for his life, so he had taken to living with the boys out on the range, wearing a large Mexican sombrero to deal with the relentless New Mexico summer sun. In the end it would be up to McSween what to do next, or at least to defer to someone with a stronger constitution to make that decision.

"As I see it, we have 3 choices" shouted Doc over the commotion, "We can stay up here hiding like sissies!". The men's objections grew even louder. "We can pull out and leave Lincoln County behind for good." he said, which was greeted by a chorus of boos. "Or, we can march back into Lincoln and fight those bastards till every last one of em is dead!" yelled Doc, which produced a cheer you could probably hear all the way to Roswell. "Alex, it's up to you. What do you want to do" asked Doc as Mc-

Sween stared quietly into the flames.

Finally after a few moments he started to speak, his voice rising in tempo and volume at each word.

"I want my house back. I want my wife back! And I want my *LIFE* back! If they want a fight, let's give them one!" screamed McSween to a cacophony of cheers, yells, and finally gunshots as the men declared their allegiance to the lawyer and their appetite to once and for all avenge the death of one John Henry Tunstall.

Somewhere in the background, away from the flames, Martin sat quietly rubbing the stock of his rifle. He'd read all the books, he'd seen the movies. He knew it was July and he knew what was coming. The Five Day Battle of Lincoln was about to commence and the war would be coming to a swift and deadly conclusion. He thought about the many comments he'd read on the Billy the Kid message boards about how the war would have turned out differently if just one of the keyboard heroes had been allowed to participate. They expounded on tactics that would have turned the tide of the battle in the Regulators favor. They surmised that *they* could have won the war and vanquished the House of Murphy to a historical footnote…if only given the chance.

Martin thought about Billy and about Bachaca's book. Surely Billy would have scanned the pages to find out how the battle unfolded? He must already know what fate McSween would face? Would this be the history changing, defining moment when Martin's careless act of leaving his book in the past would actually change it? He glanced over to the young man, whose back was to Martin. The firelight flickered, illuminating his silhouette. Martin saw the protruding ears and the sloping shoulders just like in the famous tintype, yet this Billy was a few mere feet away from him. What drove this young outlaw to act as he did? Hell, thought Martin, what drove him to care at all about Martin Teebs? They had so little in common it was almost as if they were a different species. Billy was fun, jovial, full of life. His confidence was on display every time he opened his mouth. He seemed to fear dying not at all yet had an incredible zest for life at the same time. Everything Billy was, Martin was not. Perhaps this was a classic case of opposites attracting, reasoned Martin. His mind twisted and turned, trying to make sense of the coming fight. If Billy did indeed intend to change the course of history, it would have to be now, he thought. What good would it be to have a book of your own future and not use it to save your friends? His head swooning, Martin turned off all such thoughts, fearing they might get him killed from lack of attention to the task at hand. He vainly wished for his new company iPhone so that he could logon to the message boards and let the digital Regulators know he was about to participate in the infamous Five Day Battle. Had he been able to, he knew he'd instantaneously get 15 comments telling him exactly what he should do and why he should do it....all conflicting with one another. Internet experts were many, but common sense among them was in short supply. He looked around the fire at the real Regulators. Real men who would fight and die for a cause they believed in. Martin suddenly felt very alone among the throngs of well armed men. He wasn't really a Regulator, just some modern day shmo who somehow happened upon them. He smiled slightly, imagining that the keyboard warriors would be pissing their pants if they were in his place. The thought calmed him as he prepared for war.

Martin realized he was about to get a front row seat to the most gruesome battle in the history of Lincoln, New Mexico. A number of these men were going to lose their lives, and he just hoped *his* life wasn't about to come to the same tragic end.

52

It was July and the living was easy. At least that's what the familiar refrain was for schoolteachers like Carl Farber. With 2 solid months off from teaching, Farber again scraped what little money he could together and booked the cheapest economy flight to Albuquerque.

It was July, and if his instincts were right, he'd be able to flip open the pages of his manuscript to July 1878 and wind up in the middle of Lincoln, and in the middle of the 5 Day Battle. Farber salivated at the chance to see that punk Billy and his prissy friends run for their lives out of the burning McSween house. He was even hopeful he might find a way to get in on the action. While his motives were to simply expose Billy for the coward he was, Farber wasn't completely against changing history, if such things were even possible.

As his plane descended towards Albuquerque, he let the cool air streaming from the overhead vent wash over his receding hairline and blow his thoughts 3 hours to the south, to the capitol of Lincoln County. He had a date with destiny, and a front row seat to see Billy mess his drawers as he ran and jumped into the Bonito desperately leaving his friends behind to die.

"Who knows," thought Farber, "maybe I can end that little bitch's life once and for all…and save Garrett the trouble?"

53

Having nothing to do with the scorching July temperatures in the high mountain valley, the heat coming off the walls of the McSween house was unbearable to Martin Teebs. A fire roared in the kitchen, and had been slowly spreading through the U shaped adobe all day. McSween's plan to take back his home and his life suddenly looked foolhardy. While the Regulator forces numbered almost 60 they were inefficiently spread throughout town. With less than 20 in the McSween house, Dolan's forces had pinned them down, and then called Colonel Dudley from Fort Stanton to "keep the peace & protect women and children". While Dudley's motives might have been pure, his placement of a powerful Gatling gun aimed straight at Martin and the rest of the Regulators seemed less so. Strategically, Martin and the Regulators could barely fire on any of Dolan's men, as the risk of hitting soldiers was too great. Waging war against the likes of Sheriff Peppin and Jimmy Dolan was one thing, but fighting a war with the US Army was quite something else, and well beyond what the McSween faction had signed on to.

Early in the day three men made their way up from the Bonito and after a number of tries, finally lit the kitchen of McSween's home on fire. Martin saw them retreating and was shocked to see none other than Carl Farber among the ragtag group. Once Farber reached the tree line, he looked back, spied Martin, and flipped him the middle finger as he smiled malevolently. While Martin would have welcomed the opportunity to put a bullet in his rival, poking a rifle out of the window might invite Dudley to rain hell from the Gatling upon the men in the house. With his mind swimming at the possibility of death, losing Rosita, and/or burning alive, Martin could only truly focus on one thing.

"Five days!" he fumed to himself, "I've been in here five days!" Arriving on Thursday, and storming Lincoln on Friday morning with Billy and the boys, Martin understood the gravity of his situation. It was now Tuesday. He'd surely lost his new job, Lilly would have an all-points bulletin out for him, and the detectives would easily track that he flew not to Newark, NJ after his sales training, but to Albuquerque, NM. "Nice friggin work Martin!" he chastised himself again, "Killed a man, lost your job, cheating on your wife, lost that damn book, and now you're going to roast like a Thanksgiving turkey. Nice damn job!" Martin clapped his hands together as if giving himself a macabre round of applause for the effort.

Alexander McSween had been sitting silently in the corner, accepting that this would likely be his last day on earth. He couldn't help noticing the big man next to him seeming to come unhinged, wildly talking and gesticulating to himself. As a Christian he figured he should at least provide what little comfort he could. "Hey, Martin. It is Martin right?" asked McSween gently.

Martin snapped his head around, having almost forgotten that there were 20 other souls about to perish who couldn't care less that he had gotten a free bump to an economy plus seat on his flight from LA. "Huh? Yeah, oh yeah. Martin Teebs." he replied.

"Listen Martin, I appreciate you and all of the guys coming back here. To be honest this is a little more than I expected to happen. I think maybe I miscalculated?" asked McSween with a pained look on his face.

As he absorbed the understatement of the year, Martin looked around at the glum faces. All glum except for Billy who was excitedly gesturing to Doc, smiling his crooked smile the entire time. Calm and collected, Doc Scurlock nodded his head a time or two, shrugged his shoulders, and finally patted Billy on the back. Unbeknownst to all in attendance, control of the Regulators had just been handed over to a 17 year old boy.

"What's he so excited about? Dying?" asked Martin as he gestured toward the young man. McSween couldn't come up with an answer, as the thought of dying and leaving his wife Susan behind was too much to bear. A few tears began to drop from the lawyer's eyes, making Martin feel bad for bringing it up. Billy strode up to Martin and McSween and crouched down between the two men.

"Hey Teebsie!" said Billy with a devilish smile as he patted Martin heartily on the back, "You remember when you said you was willing to die with me?"

Martin did indeed remember that conversation but was hoping he never had to pay off on the promise. "Yeah?" he ventured slowly and carefully.

"Well today you jest might get your chance!" laughed the young outlaw, "We's making a break for it as soon as it gets dark. Get your balls up Teebsie, and Alex, you're coming too. Do whatever you want with your balls!" Billy's joke made him laugh so hard he started to tear up as well, but for reasons far removed from McSween's.

As Billy scooted away Martin pondered his book. Clearly Billy had not intervened in history, at least as of yet. Everything about the Five Day Battle had played out exactly as history said it would, save for the fact that he and Farber were apparently there. Since neither a Martin Teebs nor Carl Farber appeared in any historical text of the Lincoln County War, Martin was less sure of what became of either of them. He looked sadly upon McSween, knowing that the man's fate had already been sealed. Martin only wished to be well clear of the house when McSween make his fateful pronouncement that he would never surrender.

"Alright, listen up!" yelled Doc over the crackling flames, "When the sun gets outta sight we're breaking out. Kid leads the way. We go out the back door, across the yard, and get your ass down to the Bonito right quick, or they might shoot it off of ya!"

Billy, always appreciative of a good joke, or bad one, laughed heartily again. "Yeah Doc!!" the boy yelled over the murmurs of the others, "Let's get on out so we can git us a hot supper in Patricio! If we don't, we'll *be* the hot supper!" Against the overwhelming odds they would all die, Billy couldn't help but laugh again at his joke. With the flames tickling the southern walls of the room, the men tried to will the sun into going down as quickly as possible. When it finally dropped in the western sky, the men lined up in groups of 2 or 3. Always in the lead, Billy was willing to go first and draw the fire of Dudley and Dolan's boys. Martin and McSween stood last in line, with the flames now licking their boot tips. It was as if the fires of hell themselves had come to claim the men, and McSween carried a worried, pensive look.

Finally, Doc gave the signal and Billy and 2 of the men went fast and hard to the wall of the yard and over it into Bonito Creek. Nary a shot was fired, and Martin perked up. Perhaps the plan would work? Even without his trusty book, Martin knew that McSween was a dead man, but there was no book written about his own history, so the outcome wasn't at all certain.

Doc and his men went next, again making it over the wall and into the creek. As the line inched forward, McSween's face became a terror and he pulled Martin close. Just before the little Martin group was going to make a run McSween leaned in close. "Martin, I'm going to give myself up. Fight this in the courts. You should too. At least we'll be alive." implored McSween.

Remembering the woodcut picture in one of his books of McSween being cut down in a hail of bullets, arms flailing to the sides, Martin tried to choose the right words to dissuade Alex from his plan. "Ummm, maybe let's stick with plan number 1? You know, maybe not throw the Hail Mary right here?" said Martin.

McSween quickly shook his head, "No, no! This is better. You *have* to trust me Martin. This is going to work out just fine. Follow my lead." The confidence with which McSween spoke disarmed Martin. He reasoned that in history, he hadn't been in Lincoln, yet here he was….so perhaps things could change. Maybe Alex's plan would work? Maybe he should just "follow his lead" and see if he could find some other way to have Lilly crucify him back in present day? Martin's mind was a twisted mess, unable to process which course of action would allow him the chance at seeing Rosita again?

As he played on the possibilities, young Harvey Morris yelled out "Let's go!!" and ran quickly into the backyard. Without a thought, Martin and McSween followed just as a huge fireball erupted from the house, lighting up the backyard and all of its inhabitants. Dolan's men fired wildly into the crowd dropping two men right at Martin's feet. Young Morris laid near his boot, a gaping hole in his head where his right eye used to be. In the melee, Martin fully expected a .45 slug to put him out of his misery in both present and future, but surprisingly, none came. After a few seconds McSween threw his hands up and yelled "I am McSween, and I shall surrender!". As if by magic, the shooting stopped, the quiet only broken by the sound of flames consuming what was left of the adobe, and the soft groans of the dying Morris.

Caught unaware, a few paces away, Martin slowly raised his hands too as McSween slowly craned his neck around to the big man. With a maniacal smile way too big for the situation, McSween, seemingly losing his grip on reality, took a last look at his dead law student Morris, and then whispered to Martin, "Watch. This." Turning his head back toward the street he gave Martin one last glistening side eye and loudly proclaimed "I shall NEVER surrender! Get em Martin!!"

The volley of gunfire that erupted must surely have matched that of Pickett's Charge, as McSween was hit at least 7 times. His body spun around to face Martin who look horrified as the dying man fell into his arms. With a strange look of disappointment on his face, his eyes implored Martin to lean in as he said in his dying breath "Martin, you really suck at this job."

More gunfire raged from the street as Martin used McSween's body as a human shield to get to the wall. Throwing the lawyer down in the vacant lot leading to the now defunct Tunstall Store, he slid over the wall and tumbled quickly down the hill and into the creek. The sounds of flagging gunfire, flames, and cheers rang in his ears as he ran to the east to find Billy and the rest of the boys who'd miraculously escaped the inferno.

54

What was left of the Regulators sat around a huge campfire in the hills above San Patricio. It was late, or maybe early the next morning, no one could seem to tell. The men were dirty, hungry, bloody, and furious about McSween's murder. As Doc tried to get the men to quiet down so they could discuss what to do next, Martin made his way to the fire. His shirt was covered in Alex's blood, and he was muddy from slogging through the creek. Luckily, Billy had sent a few of the boys back to help whomever else made it out of the house to get a mount and get the hell out of Lincoln.

While Martin had been a firsthand witness to Brady's execution, and had himself blown the brains of Matthews all the way to Tularosa, he'd never been as up close and personal to death as he was with McSween. Despite Alex's odd choice of strategy, Martin still felt bad he didn't perform better when the heat was on.

"C'mon Teebsie, sit right up here at the fire" urged Billy. Martin sighed heavily and stepped between Doc and Billy, settling down on a log. "This man right here," said Billy clapping Martin on the back, "is a real warrior. You there, trying to fight off that mob all by yourself and save Alex. That's some stuff of legend Teebsie."

Doc assented "That's damn right. A real Regulator!" Cheers came from around the fire as Martin saw many of the familiar faces he'd only heretofore seen in books. There was the slim faced Charlie Bowdre, tall and lanky Tom Folliard, the Coe brothers, and more. Martin was struck by the fact that no one seemed to know that he was about to surrender and hadn't as much drawn his gun. The cheering went on as the men looked admiringly at him. Martin started turning red from embarrassment, knowing if they knew the real truth, they'd have probably left him to be shot to pieces in Lincoln, just like Alex.

Just then, two horses came trotting up the hill. Billy, always the good friend, had seen to it that someone went to fetch Rosita. As she approached the fire she saw Martin covered in mud and blood, but obviously alive. She let out a slight gasp and quickly slid from the horse, running into Martin's arms.

"*Martin! Oh Martin*, you are alive!" she cried and sobbed into his shirt, "I was so worried when I saw Mr. McSween surrender, and when you put your hands u….."

Before she could finish Martin whisked her away from the Regulators with a loud "Whoa! I'm fine." Knowing she was about to spill the secret that wasn't going to ingratiate him with his friends, he quickly pulled her away towards a large tree where he carefully sat her down. The men quickly lost interest in the spectacle and went back to their discussion. Only Billy gave one last, long questioning glance back.

"Oh *Martin*, you are safe. I was so scared you would be dead" she sniffed through her tears. Martin wrapped his arms tightly around this woman that for some reason, had grown to love him. He felt, at the moment, fiercely protective of her, and as in love as he'd ever felt before with anyone in his life.

"I'm fine Rosita…I'm fine." he gently replied as he stroked a wisp of hair from her face.

"No more fighting, please *Martin*?" the raven-haired beauty asked, "Mr. McSween is dead. There's nothing more to fight for, *si*?"

While Martin knew from history that she was right, he also knew he was living in some slightly altered version of history. He wanted to be truthful with Rosita but wasn't sure he could. Finally, he decided that while the fighting might somehow go on, he wanted to be done with it. He'd tasted enough bloodshed and death to last this lifetime, as well as the one he was living over a century in the future.

"No more fighting my love," he said, "I just want to stay here, with you."

"Oh *Martin*, this makes me so happy. Now we can live here together *si*? Forever…*por siempre.*" she whispered softly into the night.

For once Martin didn't have to carefully choose his words. This felt right. This was the man he always imagined he could be. He offered, "Yes Rosita, there's nothing more in this world that I would like to do."

His words seemed to melt Rosita as she turned into him, their lips greeting in a long, deep kiss. He felt an insistence in her movements that he hadn't felt before. She pushed him firmly back against the tree and deftly removed his gun belt. The distant sound of

Billy and the boys recounting their escape faded and fizzled into the night. Somewhere in the back of Martin's brain, he remembered Lilly, but she seemed a world and another lifetime away. Rosita tugged at the buttons on Martin's pants as he slid his hands under her skirt and up to her thighs. Rosita let out a soft moan as she slid higher on her lover's body and allowed him to lose himself inside of her. As they consummated their love, Martin Teebs officially became an adulterer….almost 100 years before he was even born.

55

The rising sun cut through whatever meager shade the tree limbs provided, waking Martin from a very sound sleep. He stiffly moved his neck from side to side to get his bearings and immediately looked for Rosita. There was no sign of her, nor was there any sign of the Regulators. For that matter, there was no sign of a campfire, logs to sit on, whiskey bottles, or anything that might prove to him he was even in the same place as he fell asleep.

Martin groaned as he willed himself up from the dirt, his back aching from the hard earth. Everything around him looked the same, yet different. His mind was having trouble understanding what had happened until he heard the unmistakable sound of a jake brake on a tractor trailer roaring westward on US 70.

He was back. And he was gone. All at the same time.

A heavy weight hung on Martin's heart. He only wished he could somehow will himself back in time to be with Rosita once again. After last night, Billy and the boys had stopped making fun of him, and now saw him as one of their own. In Lincoln, in 1878, he was someone. A man to be reckoned with. A man in love, and a man that just might have impregnated the woman who yearned only to be with him for the rest of their days. Cursing the cruel twist of fate that had him fall asleep with the woman of his dreams in his arms, yet wake with them empty, he cast a last, sorrowful glance around the remote hilltop.

Martin sighed and began walking down towards the road. Having lost yet another day to the past, he realized that aside from an APB, Lilly most likely had a private detective looking for him too. Maybe she'd even chosen a coffin for him and ordered invitations to his 'celebration of life'? He wondered if Mr. Talbot would even listen to any explanation of why he never returned to work. He vaguely crafted a tale where he hit his head at the B&B and was lost in a fog of amnesia for a few days. The story was so lame that Martin decided he would be embarrassed to even tell it.

Walking to the road Martin simply decided he was going to have to take his medicine. Lilly would get the house, of course. Martin would have some crappy one-bedroom apartment. Money would be an issue so he'd have to find another job to park himself at for the next 17 years or so. At least he'd have time with his Billy the Kid books and movies to really immerse himself in the past. Maybe, if the spirits of good fortune shone upon him, he could find a way to get back to 1878 and to Rosita. While he tried to cheer himself up with chipper thoughts, deep down Martin knew his life was about to implode.

Catching another truck roaring down the highway, Martin stuck out his thumb and to his surprise, the truck stopped. The driver looked at his clothes and blood stained shirt warily, but smiled with the one good tooth he had left and told Martin to hop in. Making their way to Lincoln, Martin asked to be dropped by the side of the road near the old cemetery. There'd be no one around at this time of morning, and he hoped at least that his modern-day clothes where somewhere near the tree he left them. Mr. one tooth gave him a wave and nod and blasted Martin with a jet black stream of diesel exhaust as he made his way west.

Trekking to where he remembered his clothes being, he searched only for a few moments before finding them, in much better shape than he assumed they would be after sitting in the elements for 6 days. Martin quickly dressed and began walking toward the Patron House to answer the many questions he knew would be waiting for him. He half expected to see blue flashing lights and the scurry of news reporters talking about the missing tenderfoot from New Jersey. Martin was mildly surprised that there seemed to be no such effort taking place on his behalf.

As his sneakers crunched on the gravel driveway, Darlene came flitting out of the house, waving at him insistently. Her breasts threatened to escape the flimsy bond of her tank top with each bounding step.

"Here we go Martin" he said to himself grimly.

"Martin! Hey, there you are!" came the warm greeting from his hostess, "That group left before breakfast, so I just cleaned up real quick and put your bag in the casita."

Stunned and not understanding what was happening, Martin could only manage a befuddled "huh?" to Darlene.

"Your stuff is in the Casita hon, you can go on ahead and settle in." said Darlene.

Martin swung his head from side to side, still trying to find out where the sure to be hidden camera must be located. "What day is this?" he asked carefully.

"Martin. Have you been working too hard? Maybe that sales job is too much for you," joked Darlene, "Why. it's Thursday dear…you've got about an hour to relax before lunch is ready. Ok?"

Thursday? Martin couldn't believe it! This had to be some kind of joke. Could it be that he spent 6 days in 1878 and yet only a couple of hours had passed in real time? No losing his job? No explaining to Lilly? No crappy apartment? What luck, he thought. The unexpected turn of events had him off center, but he composed himself with a silent thank you to whomever was pulling his time travel strings.

"Um, yeah. That sounds great Darlene. I just kind of lost myself out there doing research is all." he assured Darlene as she smiled and made her way back to the main house.

"Martin Teebs, you lucky sonofabitch," said Martin to himself, "you skated by on this one." He breathed a huge sigh of relief and made his way to the casita. A long hot shower would wash what was left of McSween, and Rosita off of him.

56

Martin spent most of the rest of Thursday in his room reliving the incredible events of the day, or the six days, that he had just lived through. A passing question occurred to him. Since he'd lived 6 days in 1878, was he actually six days older in 2020? If he continued on his backwards trips in time, might he one day be a grizzled and gray, broken down old man, but still only celebrating his 47th birthday with Lilly in New Jersey? Surely someone would notice Martin's rapid aging in his present time. Surely someone would say something, wouldn't they? If Martin escaped to Rosita for say, a year, but only a day passed in 2020, how would he explain his ZZ Top-ish beard that suddenly appeared overnight to Lilly and his friends?

On Friday he cautiously emerged from his casita and carefully checked what century he was in. Satisfied that he was in present day, he walked toward the main Patron house only to be greeted by the 1000 megawatt smile of one Dallas Jones. "Hey Martin! Good to see you buddy," boomed the actor turned B&B proprietor, "Darlene told me you were back in town."

Martin inspected the man from his glowing white teeth, to his chiseled pecs, and finally to his boots. The guy had it all put together, Martin thought to himself. "Hey Dallas, good to see you again" said Martin as he stuck out his hand, "How'd the audition go?"

Momentarily surprised that Martin knew he had been back east, Dallas recovered enough to answer, "It was a guest role on some soap opera thing. I'm not sure I'll get it, but I should know in a few days."

"So just in and out of NY then?" asked Martin genuinely.

"Yep," smiled Dallas, "there was a lot of in and out…for sure." Dallas seemed to laugh way too hard at his own joke but Martin couldn't comprehend why. He looked carefully at his host trying to figure out how to, or even if to continue this conversation. Never one to let a silent moment rest in peace, Dallas piped right back up.

"So, what brought you back? You missed me, didn't you?" joked Dallas.

"Ummm, sure. Kind of. Well, I did miss Lincoln." replied Martin, not wanting to hurt the man's feelings and not entirely sure the question had been a joke. "Hey Dallas," he continued, "can I ask you something?"

"Sure hombre, shoot."

"Did you ever feel, like, out of place? I mean, were you ever in a place that was fine, but suddenly it didn't feel fine anymore? And then there's this other place that's new to you, but you feel right at home. Is this making any sense?" asked Martin.

Dallas studied Martin's face, making sure that the big man was actually talking about a geographic place, and not something like, perhaps….Lilly? "Sure do," came the reply, "when Darlene and I moved out here from LA it was after spending only a few days in Lincoln. We just fell in love with the place, and with the people, and decided this felt more like home than Cali ever did."

Martin digested the vision of Dallas cruising around in his Porsche on Mulholland Drive while his magnificent teeth outshone the California sun.

"Yeah, I guess something just drew me here. Once I got to Lincoln I felt like I'd been here for 100 years." said Martin partly to Dallas but mostly to himself.

"Well, our door's always open to you Martin. Next time, bring Lilly too, huh?" said Dallas as he popped Martin lightly on the shoulder and bounded into the house.

Martin's current desire didn't have anything to do with Lilly, however. His clean and clear memory from just the day before was of making love to Rosita and it throbbed at his brain, among other body parts. He wondered if she was already pregnant, being as they'd only done it that one time. They MUST have had more time together, since Martin had spent 10 years trying to get Lilly pregnant with no good result.

Lilly…his wife. The thought pushed into his brain, and demanded Rosita move aside, at least temporarily. What in the hell was he doing? He had just committed adultery with a woman who was born well over 100 years before his wife. He couldn't seem to make sense of that fact and wondered if he was truly guilty of any infraction? If some time court convened, could Martin plead that since he really didn't yet exist in 1878, then his indiscretions didn't either? He and Lilly started out with a good, solid marriage, but time and tide had chipped away at the romance. Martin knew that he was mostly to blame. His recent parole from his 17 year sentence in cubicle #31 only highlighted the fact that he was far from a go getter, and probably wasn't the type of man that Lilly hoped he'd be. Lilly was in a league, or perhaps two above Martin as well. Beautiful, smart, driven. Those qualities made Martin want to be a better man when they were younger, but recently just made him feel he'd never measure up anyway, so what would be the use of trying?

Kids? Sure, at some point they both wanted kids, but as their 30's faded into their early 40's it was too late. They both decided while sitting around the dining table one evening that it was time to give up the ghost. Neither of them wanted to bring a screaming newborn into the quiet they'd created in their home. Martin for sure didn't want to be a 60-something dad using his walker with tennis balls on the legs to attend his son's high school graduation. So, the rule of the day, during the very infrequent love making sessions they had, was that condoms would always be used…just in case. Martin sometimes felt angry at the little foil packs, thinking that if he and Lilly hadn't gotten pregnant by now, it was surely not to happen no matter what. Still, he went along because on most things, he felt Lilly was right. Even if she wasn't, she could usually force Martin into making the decision that she wanted, the trip to Lincoln as one notable exclusion.

Kids, he thought again. At this very moment, in a fold in time 140 or so years distant, Rosita Luna might be carrying little Martin Jr.? Martin had seen the picture, so he knew it was true. A son, thought Martin…and a Jr. to boot! The thought of the boy was almost as exciting as the thought of bedding down with Rosita again. Before he knew it, something in Martin's crotch stirred and prompted him to get up. With a deep sigh he walked into town, hoping to find some reliable portal back to 1878. He knew Rosita would be waiting for him, and he knew that he liked that idea.

Hour after hour passed as Martin walked around buildings, bumped into trees, quickly turned around to see if he could spin himself back in time, but all to no avail. By 2pm he had to admit that he was hungry and started trudging back toward Patron's. Along the way he decided that he'd had enough action for one trip. He'd call the airline and see if he could fly home tomorrow, which would save him the lie of telling Lilly that his non-existent flight had been cancelled.

A sense of calm came over him in indescribable fashion. Somehow Martin knew he'd be back in Lincoln and that he would once again see Rosita. He knew now that 1878 wasn't going anywhere and that he should spend some time shoring up his marriage before he went any further and weakened it. His new job had provided him exactly what he hoped it would: a path to New Mexico, and at least this time, into Rosita's waiting arms. He walked up the stairs into his casita, picked up his phone, and booked himself on the first flight back to Newark the next morning.

57

The Albuquerque Sunport was bustling on this early July Saturday morning. Throngs of vacationers both coming and going choked the tiny airport. While Martin expected a quiet hour or two before his flight boarded, he was thrust into a whirlwind of crowds, crying babies, service dogs, and restaurants serving basically everything with something called 'green chile' on top. As he made his way to the gate, he looked in vain over the sea of humanity for an empty seat. People were lying on the floor and standing against walls as a last resort. Just as he was about to give up, an Asian couple quickly grabbed their bags, realizing they were at the wrong gate as their flight had called for final boarding.

Settling heavily down in the now warm seat, Martin didn't notice someone else making their way down the aisle to claim the other one. He looked up, shocked, and couldn't help himself. "Oh no!" he said to a smiling Carl Farber, "You? You have to sit here? Go sit somewhere else, would you?"

Farber grinned an idiotic grin before saying, "Hey pop tart! Fancy seeing you here."

Martin fumed as Farber adjusted himself into the chair. Now he was stuck for an hour next to his arch enemy, and wondered whether to argue with him, or try the silent treatment. Farber didn't wait to find out Martin's next move. "Hey, do your armpits get cold from the draft when you're standing with your hands up next to that dumb lawyer?" teased Farber, a mocking smile spreading across his face.

Incensed, Martin fired back in an angry whisper "What the hell is wrong with you!? Men died out there. You think this is funny?"

"Hey," replied Farber, "I didn't change history, I just watched it go down…just like that lawyer!" Farber laughed mightily at the joke as Martin stewed. Finally, Martin decided he'd rather stand than sit next to the vile piece of crap he judged Farber to be. As he began to gather his things, Farber grabbed his arm, "Hey, wait. I'm just kidding. C'mon, we don't have to be enemies here too, do we?" Martin glared at Farber, and at the completely full seating area, and decided he had no choice but to coexist for another hour.

"So, twinkledink how are you liking old Lincoln?" asked Farber.

"Twinkledink? Are these even insults? Where do you get these things?" asked Martin with enough condescension that it put Farber on guard.

"I'm a high school history teacher," shot back Farber, "I hear these kids all day. I guess I just picked a few up. Ok, Mr. Rogers?"

Martin mouthed the words Mr. Rogers and shook his head. He was almost feeling sorry that at least in a battle of words, Farber would very likely fall quicker than McSween did. The thought that he could certainly beat Farber at something abated his anger just a little bit.

There was *one* burning question that Martin was dying to ask Farber. Being as they were probably the only two people at the Sunport that were traveling back and forth in time, Martin decided it might be now or never.

"Hey, can I ask you a question?" he said cautiously.

"Sure. Doggy style, no doubt. You?" came the satisfied reply from Farber.

Martin was exasperated at how unlikable the man was. "Not that you moron!" Martin barked at him. Farber, looking slightly wounded offered, "Ok, what then?"

"How do you, you know," Martin hesitated because the question sounded so stupid, "go back in time? Like, how does it work for you?"

Farber looked straight at Martin and said, "I just open my book to the page and time I want, and I'm there. Why, how do you do it?"

Martin hesitated but figured he wasn't giving away any family secrets, "Well, sometimes it's a cold breeze, or fog that blows through. One time I had to get hit by a car, another time I got run off the road by a truck. It's always something different."

"Oh boy, you watch too much TV dude. That car thing was classic though. Top notch." laughed Farber with a pinched little smile.

Curious if Farber's choice of book might help him be more regular in his time travels, he inquired, "What book is it that you use?"

Farber reached into his bag and hauled out his copy of the manuscript. He tossed it heavily on Martin lap. "Check that out Chico."

When Martin read the title, he exploded. "*Coward of Lincoln County*! Are you kidding me? You're writing this piece of shit?" demanded Martin.

"I'm setting the record straight. So yeah, read it and weep tiktok." smirked Farber.

Tempted to see if Farber had written about him in the book, he decided not to give him the satisfaction of even looking. "Billy's more of a man at 18 years old than you are at what, 80?" said Martin as he threw the manuscript and the insult back in Farber's lap.

"Oh, screw you porcupine! You saw that coward run and leave your lawyer friend to be shot up like Swiss cheese. He probably left you too! If Dolan and that band of drunkards could shoot straight, you wouldn't even be here now. Face it, he's a coward, and you're a fool for following him!" exclaimed Farber.

Martin stewed in silence for a few moments and finally spoke, "Let me know when your book comes out, I'll gladly buy a few copies to wipe my ass with."

Farber shoved the manuscript back in his bag, wondering if the verbal gunfight would continue. Martin spied a child getting up and walking away from a seat nearby. "Go. There!" he said, pointing at the now vacant chair, "Get the hell away from me…and stay the hell away from my friends!"

Farber began to form a response, but people were starting to stare at the two men as their argument escalated, and he decided to end today's match, calling it a draw. With a last, parting look at Martin, he dragged his bags over next to a very large woman eating an overstuffed green chile burrito. Farber only hoped that they wouldn't be seated together when the burrito made its inevitable exit later in the day.

58

Lilly was pleasantly surprised to see Martin a few hours sooner than expected. If she was suspicious of his travel or what he'd done, she certainly didn't show it, planting a deep wet kiss on him as he walked in the door. "Hey babe!" she exclaimed as she hugged the big man tightly, "how was the trip?"

Martin, taken aback at a show of affection from Lilly he hadn't seen in a decade or more, cautiously shot back , "It was good. Learned a lot. I think I'll like this sales thing."

Lilly held him for a moment longer before letting him go with a big smile. "My big, sexy salesman" she purred, "it's so good to have you back."

Martin's brain attempted to make sense of this new, improved Lilly. Why was she so revved up, he wondered? What had he missed that turned the clock back on their stale marriage? Could his absence have made her heart, and other important parts, grow fonder? He did have to admit that until this promotion, he and Lilly rarely spent much time apart. Perhaps this new job might give him two raises? One in his paycheck, and one in his….

Before he could even consider asking how her week was, she blurted out, "I made your other favorite, pot roast! It's a welcome home to my new executive." Lilly gave Martin one more hug and he suddenly felt very dirty. The fact that he had sex with another woman just 2 days ago left him feeling like he should shower….and maybe burn his clothes. His guilt washed over him like an ocean wave so he quickly extricated himself and told Lilly "I'm going to shower up hon. That airplane air, you know. When's dinner?"

"You've got 30 minutes tiger. Don't keep mama waiting!" she said as she slapped Martin solidly on the ass and smiled on her way out of the room.

A week ago most people barely noticed Martin, no matter how big the crowd. Now, suddenly he seemed in demand by women both past and present. First Rosita and now Lilly. Hell, thought Martin, he could probably get Darlene Jones now with his newfound gravitas, if he wanted. This must be what movie stars feel like, he thought. The turn of fate confused him, and even scared him a little, but he decided the best course of action was to just go with it. The shower's warm water washed any thoughts of Rosita away, at least temporarily. With visions of pot roast and fingerling potatoes dancing in his head, Martin Teebs dried off, dressed, and descended the stairs to dine with his newly turned on wife.

59

Full of pot roast, potatoes, and cherry pie, Martin dressed for bed in his sensible pajamas. Lilly had retired to the en suite 30 minutes prior, most likely for a bath, reasoned Martin. The day had been long, and he plopped heavily into bed, his eyes heavy but his mind racing. His duel with Farber only solidified his disdain for the man. Martin hated the fact that Farber could also travel back in time, and seemingly without all of the machinations that Martin had to try in order to escape the present. He also hated the book. Martin knew Billy had his faults, but one of them most certainly wasn't being a coward. Billy stood tall and brave in the face of danger. If he was guilty of anything it was of being a teenager who let his whim and whimsey be dictated by hormones and whichever way the wind blew that day.

Thoughts of Rosita entered Martin's mind, but he quickly pushed them away. He couldn't be lying here next to Lilly tonight, thinking about his lover from the past. It felt like cheating. Martin ruefully smiled to himself that merely thinking about Rosita felt like cheating, while he had no such reservations lying under a tree and making love to her just a few days ago. Just as Martin was about to give himself a mental lashing the bathroom door swung open. Out poured Lilly in a black lace teddy with thigh high stockings and the highest heels Martin had ever seen in his house.

"Oh my….." whispered Martin.

"Hey big boy." teased Lilly as she traced her fingers around both of her ample breasts.

Still shocked, Martin couldn't help musing, "Would you look at that?"

Lilly clearly had gotten the reaction she wanted. Martin's mouth hung slightly open, and his eyes seemed glazed but transfixed on her body. "Yes, look at that," she said pointing to one breast, "and look at this," she said as she pointed to the other.

Martin was suddenly finding it hard to breathe. His pulse was racing and he had to take a few deep breaths to slow it down.

"And," Lilly continued, "when you're done with those, you can look at this." she murmured, pointing to the dark triangle of lace that greeted the tops of the insides of both of her thighs.

This was a Lilly that Martin hadn't known in years. In fact, Martin quickly scanned his mental memory banks and decided he'd *never* known this Lilly at all. The closest thing to a wild time he could remember was the quickie they had in college while Lilly stood leaning against her faded pale blue sedan in a Burger Chief parking lot.

Martin just stared, wondering if this was really happening. Luckily Lilly cut his wait short by turning off the lamp and climbing on top of the big man in their king-sized bed. The swish of sheets and clothes made for pleasant background music as Lilly's breathy whispers and Martin's groans began to build.

Suddenly, the light snapped on, Martin's face in a ball of confusion. Was it over? What did he do wrong?

Lilly leaned over and pulled out the nightstand drawer, deftly plucking a gold foiled condom from the box inside of it. Martin's face began to fall, thinking that this one time, he might be allowed to perform au natural.

"This time, every time, remember Martin?" said the now sensible Lilly that Martin had grown to know and like. "We're too old for kids." she said, handing him the condom with a firm nod of her head.

As much as he resented the tiny latex raincoat for ruining his fun, he grabbed it quickly and put it on before his excitement faded. Satisfied that the action could resume Lilly leaned forward and kissed Martin heavily, dragging her breasts across his face as she reached to turn the lamp off.

Darkness and pleasure raced to envelope them, as dthey each drifted off to their own little mental world. In Martin's mind, and behind his closed eyes, this was Rosita rocking her hips on top of him. He could practically smell the unique smells of Lincoln as he responded in kind. He grabbed her arms and pulled himself deeper into her. His mind's eye allowed her dark, chocolate colored eyes to gaze upon him as they both dove deeper into each other.

Behind Lilly's veil of darkness, she imaged Dallas, he of the rock hard pecs, among other things. His shining smile cut through the darkness. She rode harder and faster than she ever had before, milking the moment for all it was worth, intent on giving him the pleasure he most surely was missing from his wife Darlene.

Both in their own reality, Martin and Lilly made love to their virtual paramours. As Martin approached what would be his limit for the night, Rosita's fiery eyes beckoning him to finish what he'd started, he swung his hand to the side, knocking the lamp from the table. Both lovers, surprised by the sound, opened their eyes simultaneously only to rudely find they weren't in bed with their New Mexico partners, but in fact with each other. There was an audible and surprised "huhh!" from both of them as they awkwardly tried to avoid each other's gaze in the dark room. Their movements became less insistent, and shortly came to a not so grinding halt.

The mojo lost, Lilly kissed Martin lightly on the forehead and slid off of him saying simply, "You've had a long day, and I'm tired." Without the slightest protest Martin climbed out of bed, headed to the bathroom to fix himself, and waited long enough for Lilly to be asleep before he crept back into the room and quietly slipped under the covers. In a last lucid flash before he fell asleep, Rosita's warm smile and coaxing arms called him to her. Martin couldn't tell if he reached out only in his mind, or with his arms, but she remained just beyond his reach. Exhausted from the previous week, and from Lilly's demands, he finally feel into a deep, dreamless sleep.

60

It was Monday morning, and Martin was back on the job, his new job, from his old cubicle. Now, instead of the sterile environment he'd always been in, there were stacks of papers, reports, charts, and graphs all around him. During his weeklong absence, someone had seen to it that every outstanding task and piece of paper having anything to do with sales was piled inconveniently on Martin's desk. Walking quickly across the office, Colin couldn't wait to hear how much Martin hated his sales training trip.

"Marty!" said the chipper Colin, "how was the trip?"

After everything that had happened in the past few weeks, Martin was glad to see and talk to Colin. He represented a simpler, more routine time in life when Farber didn't exist, he hadn't killed a sheriff's deputy, and he wasn't cheating on his wife. He studied the tall lanky young man, trying to determine if he'd have been any good as a Regulator. Colin was always good natured, and his energy seemed to boost Martin during any of his dark periods. He was also a loyal friend, a fact which Martin both appreciated and felt guilty about due to his preoccupation with all things Billy and New Mexico. He looked at Colin's hands, baby soft and with nary a callous from any type of manual labor. Could he shoot, wondered Martin? He decided that shooting was a skill, one that somehow and somewhere Martin had learned, and as such Colin would surely be able to master it as well. With Colin's wide eyes and good nature Martin decided he could in fact be a Regulator. The more he thought about it, the more he realized Colin would likely fit in with Billy and the boys a lot more than he would. Martin saw in him many of the same qualities he saw in Billy and decided that if Colin ever found a fold in time taking him back to 1878, he and Billy would probably become fast friends. "Hey Colin, good to see you buddy," said Martin as he gave Colin a gentle punch in the arm, "It was good. I learned a lot. Can't wait to put it into action."

Colin peppered Martin with more questions about the travel, the types of hotels he stayed in, and if he thought he'd ever move out to California. The enjoyable banter between the two men was cut short as Talbot walked up with intent, clearly needing to speak to Martin. "I'll get you those reports in a minute Colin." said Martin, covering for his friend who walked quickly away with an official looking wave of his hand.

"Martin, I heard things went well in LA last week. That sales trainer said you picked up the pitch pretty quickly. Good job." said Talbot. Before Martin could even squeeze out a "thank you" Talbot jumped back in and continued "Listen, we've got a problem with the Murphy account. I need you back out there next week. Take a few extra days and see some other prospects while you're there. Line up some cold calls, and check with the LA office manager to see who's been in touch with us. That ought to get you at least started."

"Yes Sir" replied Martin. If he was going to add anything, the moment was lost as Talbot turned to walk away. Almost out of range, he turned back to Martin and said through a half smile "Uh, Martin, go ahead and book yourself in business class on this one. A little perk to make the trip easier." Talbot winked at him as if a benevolent uncle. And with that, his new boss was gone and Martin was left with the problematic Murphy account. The coincidence was not lost on him. Murphy and Dolan had started the Lincoln County War by killing John Tunstall, and now Martin was being summoned to fix another Murphy problem. He thought quickly through his strategy and decided that ambushing anyone with the last name of Brady would be out of the question. Was it possible that the Murphy in the Murphy account was somehow related to the iron fisted Lawrence G. Murphy? If they were, did they have any idea about the absolute chaos their jackass relative had thrown the county into? Martin decided that when he walked through their door, he'd leave any thoughts of Billy the Kid and the Lincoln County War behind, lest he wind up fighting a modern version of it with a client that he needed on his side.

Back to the west coast so soon, thought Martin. He had to find a way to stretch his trip by a day or two. He had to see Rosita. He had to, if he hadn't already, finish the job of creating little Martin Jr. The more Martin thought about Rosita's impending pregnancy and his part in it, the more he realized he was fooling himself. While making the baby that history seemed to demand was important to him, he realized that the beautiful Belle of Lincoln was much more so. He could continue to lie to himself that he was only doing 'what he had to do', or he could buck up and realize that he had fallen in love with this woman, and she was occupying his thoughts almost constantly. How much time would he get with the new (old) love of his life on this trip? With the great disparity in how time seemed to elapse, perhaps he could spend a week with Rosita? Maybe a month? Hell, maybe a lifetime? The thought of never coming back to 2020 hung in the air for a moment as Martin tried to understand the reality of that scenario. No Lilly, no house, no job, and probably no money. But, he'd have Rosita by his side for the rest of his days. The tradeoff seemed worth it to the big man. Martin's head was spinning as he looked over to see Colin giving him an air high five at his recent promotion from coach all the way up to business class.

61

That night after dinner, Martin loaded the dishwasher as Lilly puttered around, putting leftovers away. He still hadn't told her about his upcoming trip, following so soon the heels of the last one. Martin knew he'd have to book his travel that evening ,so he decided on a strategy. He'd sit with his laptop and pretend he just got an email from his boss, telling him of the need to fly to LA. That way, he and Lilly could both be surprised and angry together, which might buy Martin a pass from getting a lecture and an 'I told you so' on how much travel this new job was going to require.

Settling down on the couch he waited for Lilly to walk in before he loudly exclaimed "Ohhhh! Come on!" and clicked his tongue to the roof of his mouth.

"What? What's wrong Martin?" asked the chipper as ever Lilly.

"Oh, Talbot just emailed me. We've got problems with the Murphy account in LA. He wants me out there next week!" Martin feigned a bit of anger, trying to lure Lilly into feeling sorry for him. Amazingly, she didn't seem in the least upset by the news. She sat next to him and cuddled in closely.

"Oooooh," she purred, "my big strong salesman has to go back to LA. You must be good at this Martin!" Amazingly, Lilly didn't even bat an eye at the news. Figuring he was in the clear, Martin couldn't resist adding another layer just to show how much he really didn't want to go.

"Look at this. He says to book myself business class on this trip. So, that's something I guess." he said with a dismissive wave of his hand and a frown.

"Ohhhh, business class? That turns me on." cooed Lilly as she buried her tongue in Martin's ear.

Shocked by the response and Lilly's tongue, he inquired incredulously "Business class turns you on? Really?"

"Uhmm hmmm," said Lilly between licks, "meet me upstairs in 10 minutes Mr. Teebs, I've got something to show you." Her wicked smile convinced Martin it wasn't some 2 for 1 deal on body wash from Target, or a pack of new boxer briefs for him. Lilly left as Martin pecked away at the keyboard, routing himself through Albuquerque once again on the way home. At least he'd have a day or two to get back to 1878, if the elements would just cooperate with him. Just before he hit "book this trip" he remembered Talbot's missive and he changed the flight to business class along with the astronomically higher prices that made Martin's jaw drop.

Martin made a mental note that he probably needed a new suit or jacket. His business wardrobe was dated, and he didn't want to stick out like a sore thumb in LA, like he did when he first met Billy and the boys in Lincoln. He wondered how the Murphy account would react if he showed up in his black frock coat with his Colt strapped to his hip and his Winchester in hand. "They couldn't handle the truth." Martin said to himself, aping his favorite Jack Nicholson line from A Few Good Men.

Closing the laptop, he made his way to the stairs. Just before turning off the lights on the ground floor he swore he heard an electric buzz of a massager of some sort that he never knew they had, and a few moans coming from the bedroom Lilly must surely be waiting for him in.

62

Monday dawned bright and clear as Martin found his place in the very short boarding line for the business class section of his flight. This flight changed planes in Albuquerque, and it was going to be mentally tough for Martin to be so close to Billy and Rosita, but too far to reach them. He was halfway tempted to tell Talbot that his connecting flight had been cancelled so he could steal away for the 3 hour drive to Lincoln, but in the event Martin did come back to 2020, he assumed he'd need a job and income for the foreseeable future. As he stood daydreaming about life with Rosita, now that the war was over, his peace was interrupted by a harsh familiar voice. The man made a beeline for Martin's rear flank so he couldn't be seen approaching.

"What's up lollipop?" snickered Farber, delighted at seeing the discomfort on Martin's face.

"No! You again?" implored Martin, his anger and resentment rising like a bile in his throat.

"What's the problem dipstick? I've got more work to do back there." offered Farber.

Martin couldn't believe his bad luck. Teachers had all summer off, so Farber could come and go as he pleased, or, at least as much as his meager travel budget would allow. Martin was disgusted but getting into another airport argument with this loser wasn't going to help anything. He decided to play down to the man. "Have fun, stay away from my friends, and stay out of my way" he said firmly while wagging his finger in Farber's direction.

"*You* are giving *me* orders?" asked the incredulous Farber, having opened up a side of Martin he'd yet to see, "That's rich." Farber snickered but seethed inside. Knowing that whatever Martin Teebs did for a living paid a lot better than his teacher's salary, he looked in disgust at the 'Business Class' banner that the big oaf had parked himself under.

The new, more assertive Martin, looking at Farber's threadbare tennis shoes couldn't resist the urge to pile on, "Oh, and this is Business Class. Steerage," he said waving his hand dismissively toward the end of the line, "is somewhere back there." Farber's face turned as dark as the sky during a New Jersey thunderstorm, but he couldn't find the words to counteract the truth. He simply sneered at Martin and trudged off to join the rest of the commoners who'd all arrive, stuffed into their narrow seats, in Albuquerque at exactly the same time anyway.

63

After 4 days of sales, cold calls, and the Murphy account all sorted, Martin jetted back to the Land of Enchantment on Thursday night. He was tempted to point his rental car south at that very moment and make the 3 hour drive to Lincoln. It had been a long day however, and it was almost 9pm. He had visions of driving off the road somewhere around White Sands Missile Range and having to have the jaws of life extricate him from his rental car. Even if he did make it safely, he doubted he'd want to interrupt whatever Darlene and Dallas were doing at midnight anyway. After a restless night of sleep, he rose early and made the drive south and east through the Valley of Fires and arrived at his new home on schedule, just after 9am. The morning mountain air was cool and comforting. Even being among the historically preserved Lincoln of 2020, Martin felt a deep connection with the town. Intrinsically he knew he had even more of a history here than his brief time travels had revealed. He sometimes seemed to "see" the town as it was in the 1800's, even in present day. Martin assumed his memories from the past were somehow imprinting themselves on his modern-day brain. Looking at a non-Billy time period building, his mind could insert the historically correct one in its place. He found himself becoming his own self-guided tour operator, telling himself the many arcane points of interest that used to exist as he strolled along US 380.

After checking into his casita, he changed into his 1878 period correct clothes and walked out past the main Patron house. Dallas and Darlene spied him and gave each other a look of concern, as if their friend and guest might just have lost his mind. They'd seen some of these older men and women come thru the B&B before. They had the outfits down to the last stitch, and probably spent a good many social security checks on getting their look just right. Those people were usually part of some event however, and didn't go traipsing around Lincoln like that on any old day. Martin didn't seem the least concerned that he looked like a bad western actor about to get shot to pieces in the background of some lame movie. They ambled outside to greet him before he went off to do whatever he did all day while in Lincoln.

"Hey big boy!" said Darlene as she reached out to give him one of her famous hugs. Martin leaned in sideways so as not to touch any of his private bits to hers in front of her husband. Dallas clapped him mightily on the back and massaged Martin's neck with his thick fingers. "Good to see you again buddy." beamed Dallas with his megawatt smile. The three made some small talk while Martin looked for any escape from

PAGE 189

the conversation. He had only 2 days and he needed to find his way to 1878, and needed to find Rosita. After their standard talk about Martin's new job, about why Lilly wasn't with him, and how he should definitely attend Darlene's new erotic massage class later that day, Martin bid his hosts a farewell and walked towards the street. Just before he was out of earshot Dallas called back, "Hey Martin, here. Take one of these!" as he handed off a cigar wrapped in both pink and blue bands.

Examining the strange gift, being that he didn't even smoke Martin asked, "What's this for?" Dallas smiled his confident devil-may-care smile and replied "Oh, nothing. Just a gift. Enjoy Martin!" and he strode out of sight. Martin pocketed the gift and quickly forgot about it as he was ready to attend to more important matters. His mind was in such a peaceful state, it took him just moments to reach the main road. He closed his eyes, took a deep breath of mountain air, and allowed his eyes to reopen. Unsurprisingly, he was quickly and firmly back in the grasp of 1878. With chickens clucking, donkey's braying, and people talking as if they hadn't a care in the world, he felt like he might just have landed in Nirvana.

The Lincoln County War was over, history told him that. Martin knew the killing wasn't over however, and that thought kept him on guard. In all of his research into Billy's life and the War, he never happened upon a Martin Teebs, Carl Farber, or mention of anyone time traveling into and out of Lincoln. While Martin reasoned that the events he was experiencing were actually happening, they didn't seem to be reflected in the historical record....at least not yet. Without a book of his own history, Martin couldn't be sure if he was writing it as he went, or if his story had somehow been preordained. Making a beeline to Rosita's house, he knocked on the door to no avail. Thinking his love was perhaps at the store, he walked further west down the main street. As he passed a small space between Reverend Ealy's home and the saloon he heard a gruff voice speak out.

"Hands up you God damned Regulator!"

Unarmed and alone, Martin had little choice but to throw up his hands, and as he did the dark alley erupted in laughter. "Hahaha! Teebsie, I'm wondering if you messed your drawers!" boomed Big Jim French. Jose Chavez y Chavez joined the chorus of laughter as Martin allowed an embarrassed smile to spread across his face.

"Hey guys. Good to see you. What are you doing here?" asked Martin warmly.

The two men looked at each other for a moment before speaking, understanding the big man had no idea what had happened since they last saw him in the hills above San Patricio.

Chavez slowly offered "It's Peppin. He's got Billy. Arrested him and holding him at The House."

"What!" exclaimed Martin knowing full well that Billy's confinement at The House of L.G. Murphy shouldn't be for another 3 years.

"Yeah" said French, "he picked him up a few days ago".

Enraged that his friend was under lock and key, and probably being mistreated, Martin thundered "Let's go get him out! Where's Doc anyway?"

Again Chavez and French exchanged worried glances before Chavez answered "He's gone Martin. Lit out for Texas."

"What? Why?" implored Martin.

French answered "Said he was going to have to kill again or get killed. Wanted to leave this life behind. Tried to convince Billy to go with him too."

Martin knew how headstrong Billy was and could only imagine how quickly he would have dismissed Doc's invitation.

"Billy wouldn't go." said Chavez, pulling himself up short of saying what was on his mind.

"Why not?" questioned Martin

Chavez hesitated as if he didn't know whether to answer the question, but finally did, "He said he didn't want to leave his best friend," And then after a long pause he added, "He said he didn't want to leave you Martin".

If the whole of the Capitan Mountains had fallen on Martin in that moment, he couldn't have been any more crushed. Billy was in jail, fighting for his life, because of him…a man who should never have even been in Lincoln. He'd had an easy way out. He could have ridden along with Doc and his family, reached Texas, and gone straight. Billy could have run a little ranch somewhere, married a pretty Mexican girl, and had a passel of kids. That his only reason for staying was to protect a middling salesman from the future crushed Martin in a way he'd never felt before. Martin quickly understood that history *was* changing, and there was no guarantee that Billy would escape alive this time. "Ok guys, we need to get him out, before something happens." said Martin hurriedly, wondering where he might find his guns.

"Hold your onions Teebsie, we got us a spy in there. And ain't she coming back right now." said French as they all looked up the street to see the lovely Rosita Luna coming. With her head and body wrapped in a colorful scarf, Rosita was as incognito as the most beautiful woman in Lincoln could be. Seeing Martin as she turned into the alley, her face was alight with excitement as she leaped into his arms.

"*Martin mi amor*!" she said as she plastered his face with kisses. Martin swung her in a circle, pressing her body to his in a connection he vainly hoped he'd never lose again.

"Oh yeah Teebsie, I guess congratulations are in order!" boomed Chavez to an obviously confused Martin. Putting Rosita down she stepped back to remove the shawl and expose the very beginnings of a pregnant belly.

"Oh my God!" exclaimed Martin, "Are you? Is that?" he said pointing to her slightly rounded stomach.

"Si *Martin*" Rosita beamed, "this is our *bebe*." Time played heavily in Martin's head. He had just been here 2 weeks ago in real time, how long had it been for Rosita? A month? 3 months? It was a problem that didn't make sense to him at the moment, but something that would need to wait until the pressing matter of his friend was solved.

Martin smiled broadly and gave her a gentle but firm bear hug before French cut the impromptu baby shower short, "What'd you see Rosita? Can we get him out?"

"No. *Chivito* is chained to the floor, hands and feet. They watch him every minute. He has two guards and Billy is never alone. They search me before I go in, and they watch me the whole time. I could not even get close to him." she said sadly.

All 4 looked at each other helplessly for a moment before an idea took shape in Martin's head. He was channeling either William Shatner, or Chris Farley channeling William Shatner as he found himself blurting out in short, staccato bursts, "I've. Got. A. Plan!"

64

Martin and Rosita stood in the trees just behind and to the side of The House. Martin's plan, as it were, was stolen from history. He'd hide a gun in the outhouse. Once it was hidden, Billy would get the signal from a visitor to ask to relieve himself, where he could retrieve the gun. Martin knew he was aiding and abetting the murder of potentially 2 lawmen, but he reasoned that since history was out of order, maybe Billy could just get the drop on them and they'd surrender?

"Fat chance." he said mostly to himself as he stared at the distant outhouse.

"*Que? Martin*? Who is fat?" asked Rosita innocently.

Martin looked at the flawless brown skin, the shining dark hair, the sparkling eyes, and wondered how this amazing creature had fallen for the likes of him. The pregnancy had somehow made her look more beautiful, more radiant. If he had a million chances in his modern day to woo someone like Rosita, he'd strike out a million and one times. Less than zero sounded about right for his odds of ever having her even notice him in 2020. Still, her love for him seemed so real, so solid, that it reflected the vows that were often spoken but rarely honored in modern day, "till death do us part". He fiercely wanted to protect her, which snapped him quickly back to reality.

"Listen Rosita. I want you out of here. Go home now, please? Lock the door and don't open it for anyone but me."

"*Si Martin*, but you'll be careful, *si*? Our little *bebe* needs its Daddy." she said, lovingly smiling the entire time.

"I'll be careful, I promise." he replied and with a passionate kiss he dismissed her.

Martin crept up to the outhouse, swinging the door just enough to get inside. The smell, in the late summer heat, was overpowering. Fighting his gag reflex, Martin looked for a suitable place to hide the 1873 Colt Army revolver French had given him. The gun was loaded with a full 6 rounds, not 5 as most cowboys normally did. With no safety, a revolver with a live round under the hammer could fire if its owner fell from his horse or tripped on a step and fell forward in time, as Martin was wont to do. French reasoned that Billy might need all 6 shots to make a clean break from his guards. As Martin looked along the wall boards and around the seat, he heard the squeak of the back door of the big store opening.

"No Billy! Not yet!" he exclaimed under his breath, his job not yet done. Martin peered through the boards to an even worse sight than he imagined. Deputy Bob Olinger was making his way to the outhouse…alone. No one had given Billy the signal because Martin hadn't finished hiding the gun. It was just bad luck that Olinger's intestines decided at that moment they should be evacuated.

Olinger was a loyal man of the House. In time he would become a Deputy Sheriff of Lincoln County under Pat Garrett, and even earn a commission as a Deputy US Marshall. A big broad man with an even larger ego, Olinger wasn't even liked all that well among his friends, much less the Regulators. His sour temperament made him an ideal choice to guard the boy that Peppin had taken to calling "the scourge of Lincoln County".

"Oh shit! What do I do? What do I do?" Martin said to himself. He was left with only 2 real choices. First, he could kill Olinger himself when he opened the door. That, of course, would prompt the other guard and Peppin's deputies to rain hell on him. He doubted he'd survive an outhouse shootout, vaguely recalling the scene in "Young Guns" when Buckshot Roberts met his untimely end in the same, stinky manner. Martin's other option was in some ways worse, but at least he might live. With Olinger quickly approaching the door, Martin made his decision and slipped down into the hole. He quickly vomited as quietly as he could and hoped that perhaps Olinger might only have to piss. That hope was dashed as the large deputy closed the door behind him and farted very loudly. Olinger slipped down his pants and drawers and began to sit. Martin's world went literally and figuratively dark as the last vestiges of light were sealed out by the ample ass of one Robert Olinger.

Martin held his breath and covered his eyes and mouth with his hands as the remnants of whatever vile stew Olinger had for dinner the previous night rained down on him in wet, foul, dripping chunks.

65

Finally spying the coast being clear, Martin Teebs, covered in the excrement of everyone on the west side of Lincoln Town, exited the outhouse with great haste. He ran quickly to the trees and stripped off all of his clothing save for his underwear. Vomiting two more times and moving faster than most big men could, he sprinted across the main street and launched himself into the trickle of water that was the Bonito Creek. Martin rolled around in the cool mountain creek ,trying to wash the waste off of himself. Finally, when he felt he could do no better he crept along the tree line to where Rosita's house was and firmly knocked on the door.

"Rosita! Rosita! Open up, it's me" he urgently whispered to her.

Peering from the window Rosita quickly unlatched the door and beheld the sight before her. "*Martin*! What happened??" she said, just as a westerly breeze blew Martin's aroma towards her. "Oh *Martin*, you stink. Come now, have a bath." she said gently. Embarrassed at having his woman see him (and smell him) this way, Martin had no choice but to follow as Rosita stoked a fire to heat up some bathwater. An hour later, freshly bathed and scrubbed, Martin and Rosita lay in bed. As Martin spooned the young woman, he ran his hand lightly over her belly. Rosita threw her head back and let her hair softly cascade across Martin's face.

"A baby! I can't believe it Rosita. He's going to be perfect" gushed Martin as his hand rubbed warmth into her belly.

"He?" she exclaimed, "How could you know *Martin*? It could be a girl."

Martin, realizing he had given up a historical secret, quickly backtracked. "Yes, that's what I meant. He *or* she will be perfect." he said as Rosita pressed her back into him.

The sublime happiness and simplicity of his life in Lincoln permeated Martin's mind and his soul. He'd long since decided if he could stay here, he would. Lilly had the house, the bank accounts, the life insurance. She was beautiful in her own way too, and after mourning Martin for many, many months (he hoped) she'd meet someone new and move on to have a nice life.

His life now was with Rosita…and with his soon to be born son. That lonely picture he saw months ago at the Patron house haunted him. There sat Rosita, Martin Jr. in her arms. Her eyes were vacant and hollow as only a woman who has been abandoned can have. The fact that the picture even existed bothered Martin and he vowed to erase it, and any memories of it in the here and now of Lincoln, NM 1878.

"I'm so happy Rosita. So happy to be here with you," said Martin before adding truthfully "I've never been this happy in my entire life".

Rosita's warm skin pressed into him, and her gauzy linen blouse stretched to contain her growing breasts. She rolled over to face her lover, stared him directly in the eye and said, "*Martin*, never leave me again. *Por favor*, the baby and I need you."

Martin cupped her face and looked into her shining eyes before speaking, "Never again. Never again my love". A smile spread across Rosita's face as she pushed Martin flat on the bed. Swinging her legs over him, she straddled the big man that she now would build a life with. Without a shred of guilt Martin needed no more prompting as he eagerly made love to the woman he had already made a mother, and hoped soon to make his wife. Any last thoughts of Lilly drifted from his mind like a high desert summer breeze. This was where he belonged. Martin Teebs was finally home.

66

The quiet of the bedroom was only broken by the occasional horse and wagon heading down the main road. In his bliss, Martin had completely allowed his mind and body to accept that he was never leaving Lincoln. With Rosita lying next to him, he felt as complete and as at home as he ever had. *This*, this was the life he was destined to live. It's as if a missing piece of the puzzle of his life had suddenly fallen into place, and it felt good. A powerful hunger began to rumble in his belly and he sat up with a start. "How about I make you breakfast!?" he asked of the lovely young woman. Rosita made a curious smile aided by her head cocked to the side.

"Where do you come from *Martin Teebs*, that a man cooks for his woman? Where is such a place?" she teased.

For a nanosecond, Martin considered telling her the truth, the whole truth, and nothing but the truth. Coming clean on who he was and where he was really from. He imagined that by shedding his secret, he might shed his life in the 21st century. It was clear that Rosita already knew something was up. That day when he tripped on her front porch and disappeared must surely be burned into her memory. "I mean," thought Martin, "what kind of person just ups and vanishes into thin air?" Perhaps Rosita would understand. She'd see the sacrifices he was making to spend his life with her. He could tell her about their son, and his future. He could tell her *everything*…. Then he saw himself being hauled off to some sanitarium in the middle of the desert, dressed in a custom fitted straight jacket, and thought the better of it. Instead, he just smiled back at her.

"Now, go please. Get some water from the well, and I shall make you *desayuno*." announced Rosita, her naked body rising strongly from the bed, temporarily taking away Martin's ability to breathe. Martin began to get dressed in whatever he could scrounge together from a trunk in Rosita's room. She said the clothes belonged to her father, and by their age, Martin didn't question it. He strapped on his gun belt just in case and grabbed a bucket to fill with water.

"*Martin*, to the store *por favor*? For some butter for the *galletas*?" Rosita asked with a warm smile. Martin had no idea what *desayuno* or *galletas* was, but he was pretty sure it was going to be good. At minimum, Rosita had asked for butter in English and he suspected he might be able to get some at the Montano store, just across the street.

Giving Rosita a kiss on the cheek he left the house humming an Aerosmith tune "Walk This Way". Martin had to admit, he felt at that moment like the king of Lincoln. For once, he felt like his life was following a road map. It was as if he actually knew what he was doing…and the feeling enthralled him. Stopping outside the former Tunstall store, he began to pump some water from the well into the metal bucket.

Suddenly the peace of Lincoln was shattered by the sound of rounds being fired. There was great yelling and screaming, and Martin was sure he heard the blast of a shotgun as well. A shrill voice in the distance cackled "Hello Bob!" and Martin realized that Billy was making his famous escape. This shouldn't be happening, at least not this way. Bob Olinger was supposed to live until Billy broke out of this jail in 1881, but it sounded to Martin like old Bob was on the receiving end of 18 dimes, albeit 3 years too soon.

Suddenly from behind him he heard a voice. "You!" spat Farber, looking upon his rival.

Martin's eyes narrowed and his right fist clenched. "What are you doing here?" he said accusingly at Farber.

"Me? *You're* the one who doesn't belong here white boy!" Farber shot back.

While Martin processed the insult, Farber reloaded "You hear that shooting? That's your doing. I saw you, you crap covered coward! Those deputy's blood is on *your* hands now!"

Martin had heard enough, finally exploding, "Get the hell away from me, and get the hell out of here, or you're next!"

Farber grimaced at the big man before warning him, "Listen friend, you'd better…."

Martin let him go no further and shot back, "I'm not your friend, asshole!"

Farber took only a moment to think before responding "And I'm not yours!" and with that, he drew his gun and fired. The bullet shot wildly to the side of Martin' head as the bucket crashed to the ground, water splashing the men's boots. In return, Martin drew his gun and fired, hitting Farber in his right upper arm.

"Arrrghh! That hurts!" wailed Farber as he grasped at the wound. His eyes having gone crazy like a wounded animal, Farber lunged at the bucket and swung it at Martin's head, barely missing. Martin, gun still drawn, pondered whether to fire again and kill the man when the bucket came whizzing at his head once again, connecting firmly on his forehead with a sickening thud. Farber dropped the dented bucket and ran quickly into the trees near the creek.

Martin's world began to turn black as he fell in the center of the street. Gunshots rang out and the sound of men running pulsated in his brain. The searing pain of the blow to the head was taking him to the edge. He desperately tried to remain conscious but the lights were quickly going out. His knees buckled and he hit the ground hard. A puff of dirt rose from the road, and all that was earthly of Martin Teebs simply vanished into the thin mountain air.

Billy and French ran by just in time to see the spectacle. "Teebs! What the hell?" yelled "Big Jim" French, confused, and then turning to Billy, "Where in the hell did he go Kid?" Billy, for his part, just stared sadly at the blank spot that used to contain his friend. It's not as if this was the first time Billy saw Martin Teebs up and vanish (or up and appear from thin air), but this time felt more permanent, as if he just lost his best friend without even a chance to say goodbye.

With no time to waste and Peppin's men chasing them, Billy and French ran towards the livery where they hoped to hell that Chavez was waiting with their mounts.

Hearing the commotion, Rosita Luna had come running up the street from her house at the last moment and saw the father of her child simply vanish before her eyes. She ran to the spot screaming his name, clutching at the air, dropping to her knees and wailing for him, begging that he come back, but to no avail. No matter how hard she pounded the dusty dirt road demanding he reappear, Martin Teebs….was gone.

No one remembers how long she cried in the street, but when some well meaning friends guided her back to her house, all that was left in the street was a dented metal bucket.

67

Later that evening, as Rosita sat sadly and quietly in the darkened room, only illuminated by a candle, there was a soft knock on her door. "Rosita, it's me! Let me in" the voice whispered urgently.

Knowing that Martin would keep his promise to never leave her, she leapt from her chair shouting his name, "Martin!" she cried, lifting the bar that locked the door she peeked out hoping to see the only man she'd ever loved, yet was met by ghoulish face of one of the few she ever truly hated. Carl Farber.

"*Puerco!*" she shouted as she slammed the door closed. Just as the bar was about to slip back into position, Farber leaned his good shoulder into the door, pushing Rosita back violently. Farber stood menacingly in the door frame as she regained her balance. Rosita looked wildly around the room, spying Martin's Winchester. She lunged for the rifle at the same time Farber did. Grabbing the barrel he wrestled it away from her, levering the rifle enough times to clear every round. Tossing the rifle on the chair he spoke in menacing fashion, "Let's *not* do this, ok? You wouldn't want to spoil our good time before it even got started, would you?" Farber smiled with his yellow teeth as he pushed the remnants of his stringy hair out of his eyes. Rosita looked warily at the man who was slicked with sweat, pasted with grime, and whose eyes for some reason just didn't look, *right*. Full of sadness for Martin and anger at Farber, she spat at his shoes and hissed, "I'd rather be dead!" with a look of defiance blazing in her eyes.

Farber wasn't about to be intimidated by a 25-year-old Mexican girl, no matter how pretty she was, and coolly replied in a low and threatening voice, "Either way. Your choice."

In the flickering candlelight Rosita finally spied the bloody bandage tied around Farber's right arm. Sensing this might be her last chance to save herself, she lunged at the schoolteacher and dug her fingers deeply into the wound. A searing pain shooting through his arm and shoulder, Farber howled in pain before turning and backhanding Rosita hard across her face. She refused to go down however, standing there defiantly with a trickle of blood running down from the corner of her mouth. Carl Farber had never hit a woman before. In fact, until his altercation with Martin earlier in the day, he'd never really hit a man. His few schoolyard fights as a kid ended quickly when he got pummeled into a wailing ball of pain and sadness. It struck him that this was the first fight that he expected he was going to win. Still in the throes of pain from his bullet wound Farber grimaced and laid out the terms of his conquest to the young beauty, "This *is* happening" he said flatly, his crazy eyes dancing around the room, "it can go hard or you can just lay back and enjoy it. I strongly suggest that you enjoy it."

For the first time, fear entered Rosita's eyes, finally understanding the depth of Farber's threat, and Carl knew he'd won. He placed his good left hand to her breast and pushed Rosita down to the floor hard, standing over her while undoing his pants with his good hand. Somewhere deep in her mind Rosita silently screamed, begging for Martin to arrive and save her, but her call went unheeded. She began to thrash and scream as Farber yanked her knees apart and kneeled between them. With his left hand he tore the muslin blouse from her breasts, and then pulled her skirt down. Rosita fought for herself, her baby, and her lover Martin with all she was worth clawing her fingers deeply into his neck, his flesh peeling away in her hands, but in the end Carl Farber was too strong, and could not be stopped. His blood dripped from the wound in his neck and from Rosita's fingers as she fought to gouge his eyes out. As the drops pooled on her torn blouse, an evil look spread across his face, almost as if enjoying the pain. Carl Farber committed the most vile, atrocious act a man can to a woman, to the chorus of her screams, sobs, and constant calling for her lover.

"*Martin! Martin! Martin!*"

Martin Teebs, just 200 feet away in distance, but 142 years away in time, sadly never heard Rosita's cries and could do nothing to help her.

68

Two weeks later, Martin Teebs sat on his very sensible couch, bored and distracted. Since returning home from New Mexico he'd been withdrawn and sullen, and Lilly could not figure out why. Sitting there with his laptop he pecked away at the keys, occasionally hitting enter to search for some new bit of arcane knowledge about the Lincoln County War. With nothing new popping out at him, he tried to find ways to keep his mind off of Rosita, Billy, and anything else to do with Lincoln. The ache in him to go back was at once too great to bear, and too scary after having shot yet another man…even if that 'man' was Carl Farber. While Mr. Talbot had been happy with Martin's work, he so far had not directed his new salesman to head out west again. Martin, for his part, wasn't sure he wanted to go anywhere near Lincoln anyway. He still bore the thick scab on his forehead where Farber had whacked him back to the present. Telling Lilly he hit his head while entering the plane, he sighed in relief when she actually believed him.

In those final moments with Rosita, and after, Lincoln had become very real for Martin. The blinders had been pulled from his eyes, as to what his real life in Lincoln would be like. He was going to be a father. His friend shot his way out of jail with a gun that Martin himself provided, murdering two deputies along the way. If he were to go back, he'd have to somehow take Rosita and leave Lincoln, as he was surely a wanted man. How would he provide for his wife and child in the old west? Were there any advertising sales jobs he could apply for? Would he have to follow in Billy's footsteps and steal and gamble to make a living? Could he move them east and learn to become a farmer? The questions were many and the answers were few. Martin's mood darkened as he realized that he'd passed the point of no return and could never, ever return to Lincoln, New Mexico in 1878. To go back now would mean to inherit all of the history which he'd contributed to making. Martin now understood that his daydreams of Lincoln, Billy, and Rosita were like billowy clouds against a deep blue sky. Beautiful to look at, but prone to dissolving when things got too hot. He had seen both the incredible light of Rosita, and the incredible darkness of his own actions. Living in Lincoln, circa 1878, would not at all be the picnic that Martin had hoped it would be. It would be real life. Dirty, messy, uncomfortable, and at times amazing. Martin finally realized he'd only be trading his own reality for a much more dangerous one.

"Hey babe!" called Lilly, sneaking up behind him, which temporarily shocked Martin out of his funk.

"Oh, hey Lilly." he meekly offered in return. Lilly had sensed that Martin was different after the last trip. She didn't know what had happened but reasoned that something *must* have gone south to turn his normally happy self into the gloomy couch dweller she saw before him.

"Wanna go out? Maybe get a beer or something?" she asked in the most chipper voice she could manage.

"To where?" he asked warily.

"Ummm, how about that new Irish bar, Dolan's? I hear they've got some great beers. It'll be fun!" proposed Lilly. Martin shook his head and sighed to himself, as if he'd ever be caught dead in a place called Dolan's.

"Well, you've got to do something Martin. You're starting to become one with this couch. I'm getting worried about you." lamented his concerned wife.

"I know Lil, I know," Martin replied, "but I'm just in a funk. I guess I need a hobby or something."

Lilly, with a concerned look, inspected her husband closely, trying to figure out a way to help him, or at least prompt him to lift his ass off the sofa. "Why not call Colin? You like him, right?" she asked.

"Oh, yeah. Well, Colin has a new girlfriend and he's no longer available to do anything except talk about how hot she is." offered Martin, shooting down yet another of Lilly's grand ideas.

Martin's fingers typed "Lincoln County War" once again into the search engine, hoping that maybe he'd be directed to some portal that would explain his recent experience in this life and his past one. Nothing new seemed to appear until he clicked on "Page 2" and saw an ad under the "Events" tab. Martin's eyes lit up as he scoured the ad:

Lincoln County War Reenactors Group Forming!

Historians, old west buffs, and anyone who wants to have an old fashioned good time are encouraged to apply. Organizational meeting Saturday September 19, 2020. Glen Rock, NJ. 1pm. All are welcome!

Martin was stunned! A reenactors group right here in Bergen County? What were the chances? His mind was alight, wondering who would have enough interest in The Kid and the war to join the group? He reasoned it wasn't going to be like really being in Lincoln, but at least it would let him scratch the itch. After all, who knew more about Billy the Kid and the war than he did? Suddenly energized Martin checked his watch. 12:15. He had just enough time to eat a couple slices of cold pizza and head to the meeting. "Hey Lil, I'm gonna go to this history thing in Glen Rock today, ok?" Happy that he was going to give the couch a chance to pop back to shape after weeks of being molded to his ass, Lilly quickly agreed. She hadn't seen Martin this excited in weeks and if some boring history lecture was going to put some pep in his step, who was she to tell him not to go for it?

69

Martin slowly opened the door to suite B12 at the mostly abandoned strip mall. Peering inside he saw a number of folding chairs, a couple of tables, and not a living soul in the vacant, sterile storefront. Checking his watch, he noticed that in his excitement he was at least 10 minutes early. One of the tables had some stacks of paper, a few pens and seemingly nothing else. Martin slowly stepped in, wondering if he might possibly be in the wrong place? Just as he was about to walk outside, the sound of a toilet flushing caught his attention as the squeak of a door drew his eyes to an area behind the main table. Out walked none other than the absolute *last* person Martin wanted to see, Carl Farber. Farber was dressed in his usually ratty khakis and a plaid shirt. His right arm was up in a sling, and he winced slightly either at seeing Martin, or at the bullet hole that Martin had put in it.

Fighting the urge to run at Farber and finish the job, he instead offered, "Oh God, not you?" Martin's disdain and disappointment was clear upon seeing the man, "I should have known, I'm out of here". Muttering the word 'bullshit' under his breath, he had just started pushing the door open when Farber broke the uncomfortable silence. "Hey! Martin, wait a second. Please…?" The nearly normal tone of Farber's voice, coupled with the lack of his juvenile name calling caught Martin off guard, so he stopped and slowly turned to face the man.

"What?" said Martin grimly.

"Don't go so quick, ok?" asked Farber, "Just gimme a second." Martin raised his eyes at his bitter rival. The adrenaline coursing through his veins urged Martin to punch Farber right in the mouth, but the angelic lawyer on Martin's shoulder told him that spending a few nights in jail was not what Lilly had in mind when she urged him to get out of the house. Fighting the inner battle in his head, he flexed his fists on both hands and just grunted in Farber's direction.

"Look, that was really bad back in Lincoln. It just got too real. I got too caught up in it, you know? I'm sorry about it all. I wish it had never happened." An apology from Farber? Martin was stunned by the gesture as he gently touched the scab on his forehead and did indeed know that it got too real.

Farber continued "I can't go back…ever. What happened was just too much. But I miss it man." Farber shook his head as if trying to either regain a memory, or forget one. "I just wanted something to give me that feeling again. That rush, but without THIS feeling." Farber, smiling, held up his arm that still bore the bullet wound that Martin had so deftly given him. He winced again at the pain, which didn't escape Martin's attention. He knew that he was the one responsible for the bullet hole. He wondered, what would have happened had he killed Farber? Would anyone know? Would anyone care? How could he possibly explain that to Lilly?

Still, his rival's smile disarmed Martin a bit. "I know what you mean, I guess," he said. "I can't keep coming home like this either." he said while pointing to the ugly gash on his head.

Farber smiled warmly before speaking, "Listen Martin. Help me stay here and run this thing. Heck, just try it for this one day. After all, who knows more about the Lincoln County War than us?" Farber gave a knowing smile and Martin could only nod his assent. He thought for a few moments about it. Who could ever understand what had happened to him more than Farber? While he certainly didn't like the man, he didn't absolutely hate this new improved Farber as much as he did the old one. He could try it out for a few days or weeks and see if it did indeed scratch the itch. Fighting against his much better judgement, Martin found himself saying, "Sure, I'll give it a try. Why not?" before he could stop himself.

Farber seemed delighted with the answer and pulled up a chair for Martin behind the main table. As Martin sat down he caught a glimpse of Farber's neck replete with a handful of deep scratches in it. "Damn, what happened to you? Do you have a cat, or a lion, or something?" asked Martin. Having forgotten about the scratches, Farber shot his hand to his neck to cover the evidence, but coolly replied "Haha, no Beetlejuice. Rough sex…you should try it sometime."

Martin gave an audible "ughhh" at the emergence of the old Farber but sat down anyway as a few people gathered outside the storefront, ready to take their own trip back in time…and back to Billy.

70

"So," said Farber, "who is it that you want to portray?" Martin waited patiently while staring at the aged, tiny Asian man. Try as he might, he couldn't remember a single Asian in the history of the Lincoln County War. He had to think back to his Young Guns days to even think of Yen Sun, Doc's Celestial girlfriend. He earnestly hoped that this old man didn't want to play Murphy's concubine.

"I Beery!" said the elderly man in an Asian accent as thick as Texas toast, "I Beery the Kid! You make me Beery, ok? I be very good Kid!"

Farber stifled a laugh by coughing into his hand and turned to Martin, "Well, this is kind of your area of expertise, so….what do you think?"

In a flashback moment Martin remembered his first time back in 1878, and how the Regulators seemed to regale in teasing him about his looks and his clothes (and his wife, and getting slapped by Rosita). He vowed silently to himself that anyone who wanted to be part of this reenactor group would do so without being teased or judged. "Hey, you look like a great Billy to me. Welcome to the group Kid!" Martin said as the tiny man happily walked off to find a seat.

Farber smiled with a slight laugh as a very large black man moved down the line in front of them. He had to be 6' 5" and 275 pounds. Almost afraid to ask, Martin was the first to speak "So, who are you interested in portraying?"

In a screechy voice mimicking a line from the Young Guns II movie he responded, "I'm Doc, I'm a schoolteacher from the city of New York!" Martin snapped his head toward Farber who had to turn all the way around to avoid laughing in the new Doc's face. With a frown at his old rival/new friend Martin decided to make the call on his own. He stuck out his hand warmly and said, "Welcome to the Regulators Doc!" The big man beamed with pride at being accepted and danced off to meet the new Billy, so as to plan their conquest of the House of Murphy and Dolan, and to take over Lincoln County in the name of their employer, John Henry Tunstall.

"Wow" said Farber, "this is a trip, isn't it? I wasn't sure what to expect but it sure wasn't this. Gonna be hard to escape reality with this crew fighting the War."

"Hey, at least people are interested," reasoned Martin, "and it'll be good to be around people who like the stuff that we like, even if it's just a couple of days a month." Farber shrugged his shoulders hard enough to cause a searing pain from his bullet wound. As he scrunched up his face waiting for the pain to pass, a 5-foot-tall bald man, who was just about 5 foot round ambled up in front of the two organizers. He was wearing period clothes with a black overcoat, dark hat, a fancy silver vest, and a Sam Colt .45 snugly on his right hip.

"Howdy Gents!" announced the fat man.

"Well, hello there cowboy," offered Farber in his classic, mocking tone, "who are you supposed to be?"

The fat man looked at them with his sweaty, oily scalp and his belly doing its damnedest to break through the last good button his pants were holding onto, and said, "Why, I'm Pat Garrett of course! Duly elected Sheriff of this here Lincoln County!" This was too much for Farber to contain and he swung around in his chair, sneezing his laughs into the wall behind him and punching Martin in the ribs at the same time.

Straight faced, Martin replied "Pat Garrett, huh?" and slowly nodded his head. Before the fat man could answer, Farber leaned into Martin and whispered into his ear "More like Fat Garrett!". Farber descended into another round of laugh-coughing while Martin shot him a disapproving look. Growing impatient with the two men, the Sherriff spoke again.

"Yeah, they called him, I mean me, Juan Largo because we were so tall. Did *pretty good* with the ladies too, if I do say so myself." said Garrett with a confident smile. Finally, the dam broke as this was all way too much for Farber to handle. Without a word, he got up and walked quickly away toward the bathrooms, rather than risk a confrontation with the good sheriff. Getting Martin's nod of approval, the new Sheriff Garrett moved on down the line to confront Billy and Doc, while Farber returned and collapsed in laughter on the chair next to Martin.

"Come on man! Are you going to take this seriously or not?" Martin admonished Farber. With a huge sigh at Martin suddenly becoming a buzzkill, Farber rolled his head and his eyes and responded, "Yes, yes, yes. Let's move on." Both men looked up just in time to have their veins turn immediately to ice water, as the color drained out of both of their faces, but for very different reasons. There before them, in skintight jeans, a form fitting crop top, heels, full makeup, and the latest hot girl hairstyle was none other than Lincoln's belle, the beautiful Rosita Luna.

71

"Rosita!" the word escaped Martin's lips without a chance to even hold it back. His eyes wide in amazement, the blood began flowing in every extremity in his body. Martin's breath was shallow and his heart pounded as he tried to comprehend what cosmic event had taken place to launch the great love of his life forward 140 years, and to the exact strip mall he was in to boot. Farber had similar thoughts as Martin, but for drastically different reasons, as if the past had seemingly come to pay him the just rewards for his sins. However, no expression on the lovely woman's face betrayed that she knew either man. There was a moment of silence between the three of them, no one daring to speak first.

"I'm sorry?" the young woman finally said, "did you call me Rosita? My name's Karin."

"Ummm, no. I mean yes, I mean…well," apologized Martin, "it's just that, and I'm kind of an expert on this, you look exactly like the Belle of Lincoln, Rosita Luna. She's the….I mean she *was* the most beautiful woman in all of New Mexico. Is that who you want to portray?" he asked hopefully. Farber kept his head down and eyes pointed towards the table, still lost in his panic that this might actually *be* Rosita, coming from beyond the grave to spill his terrible secret and maybe, his blood. He glanced up at the woman once more, but she left no clues that she recognized him.

"Noooo, no, no, no, no, no, no," she replied, laughing a bit more with each word, "You think this? Me?" she continued, pointing at the other reenactors and the table full of paperwork. Her smile enveloped her entire face much the way the real Rosita's did and Martin marveled at the likeness. "Oh God no," she finished, "I brought my auntie here." With that she stepped aside and allowed her aunt Rose to step forward. Martin and Farber exchanged quick side eye glances and tapped nervously on the table. The woman, who was probably attractive many years, and many pounds ago, was stuffed into a leopard print dress that was at least 2 sizes too small. Her sagging breasts threatened escape every time she moved, and her hips swayed in unison with her darting eyes. She was a glowing orange color as if she'd spent either too much time in the sun, or not enough money on tanning lotion. Her hair, whatever color it was now, was baked, fried, and ironed into a crispy coiffe that was held together with what had to be at least a half can of hair spray. When her bright red lips spoke it was with the thick accent of someone who'd never seen Mexico, but probably had lived in the south Bronx for much of her life.

"I'm Rosita Luna bebes," she purred "wheesh one of you boys is want to win the Belle of Lincoln's heart? Eh?" She rested her hand firmly on one of her solid hips, waiting for a reply.

There was a dead silence coming from the table before Farber, unable to contain himself any longer, whispered into Martin's ear "Two pounds of sausage in a one pound pack. You win amigo, Rosita is all yours!" Farber clapped him on the back and quickly made his way towards the others, leaving Martin to rekindle his romance with the modern day version of the woman of his dreams. Martin could only look up and give a tight little smile as the new "Rosita" swayed her ample hips and batted her long fake eyelashes at him. If karma was going to punish him for cheating on Lilly, this amounted to damn near a knockout blow.

72

Two hours later, with Martin riding herd over the new crop of Regulators and townspeople, Farber made his way back to the table to begin packing up. All in all, it seemed like the first day of the Bergen County Regulators would come off as a hit and he was pleased. After a few moments he sensed the approach of someone, and was pleasantly surprised to look up and see a pretty, middle-aged woman standing before him.

"Uh, hi, can I help you?" greeted Farber with his most non-threatening smile.

"Hi, I'm Jane. Jane Taylor." the woman said while holding her hand out.

Farber gently grasped her hand with his left hand, never allowing his eyes to leave hers. "So, are you here to be a reenactor Jane?" he asked with a smile.

Jane seemed almost embarrassed but glanced around, and was glad that the people in the room seemed relatively normal. "I was thinking about it, yes," she replied, "I'm a history teacher and thought this might be fun?"

Of all the luck in the world, Farber must have corralled most of it to have this woman walk into his reenactors club *and* be a history teacher to boot. "You are?" he said with surprise in his voice, "I am too! Over at Waldwick High."

"No way! I teach here at Glen Rock. How do we not know each other?" she said with the tone that told Farber he might just be onto something. Farber shook his head in wonderment that they'd never met before while Jane continued, "I could just be some townsperson or something. It doesn't have to be anything big. I'd just like to participate. Just being among people that love history as much as I do would be fun!"

Sensing his fortunes might be turning for the good, Farber rose from his chair and guided Jane to a seat farther away from the others so they could have some quiet. "I'm Carl. Carl Farber. So nice to meet you Jane," he said, then continued "Now listen, I'm quite sure we can find someone for you to portray that's more fitting of your intellect…..and," he added after a pause, " your beauty."

Jane smiled warmly at him as they sat down and began to talk of things only history teachers could find interesting.

73

By 4pm the meeting had wound down, having gone better than either Martin or Farber had expected. They stacked chairs and folded tables mostly in silence, each reflecting on their brush with the past. Martin had forgiven Farber for his joking and taunting of their new crop of Regulators, but still, he was on guard and watchful for the old Farber showing up in time to ruin the day. Carl gathered up his papers and shuffled his way towards the door. With a last glance around, Martin walked out of the door and watched Farber lock it behind him.

"Well, that went pretty good, huh? I mean, it was better than I expected." said Farber.

"Yeah, they were nice people. It'll be a nice group I think." answered Martin.

Farber hesitated to ask the next question, knowing that there was a real possibility of rejection. He didn't want to take for granted that Martin had enjoyed himself enough, or seen enough promise in the group to continue to be a part of it. "Do you think you'll stick with it?" asked Farber with a hopeful lilt in his voice, "After all, you did get Rosita back!" Farber was back, the old annoying Farber, and could barely control his laugher as Martin shot him a disgusted look. "Hey, I'm kidding. Just kidding. Sorry man." he apologized, holding his one workable hand up as if to prove the point.

"You and that Jane looked pretty chummy. What's up with that?" asked Martin as Farber struggled with the key and his bag of paperwork.

"She's nice Martin. Really nice. I can't believe she walked in here today. Not sure I can remember when anyone has been that nice to me." said Farber. Feeling slightly awkward, Martin had no response, so he simply smiled and waited for Farber to continue. "I got her number. I think I'll ask her out to dinner. God…it's been so long since I've been on a date." Farber said, mostly to himself. "Hey Martin," he continued, "Do you think you and your wife would maybe like to double date sometime?"

Martin's thoughts were lost between the Farber that he grew to know and hate in Lincoln, and this new more vulnerable Farber. Maybe the guy just needed a break, or needed a friend, thought Martin. Maybe he was a decent guy just waiting to break out of the asshole's shell he'd surrounded himself in? In any event Martin could count the number of people he considered friends on the fingers of one hand, and still have a few fingers left over. He reasoned that he might as well give Farber a chance in the present, because he sure as hell wasn't going back to the past.

"Sure, sometime," Martin offered, "but why don't you see how it goes with you two first?"

Farber seemed content with the answer and began to walk towards his car. Placing the bag and papers on the hood he turned back to Martin one last time. The one giant elephant in the reenactor's room still hadn't been discussed. Who were Martin and Carl to portray? Of course, based on the real, raw time they'd fought each other in Lincoln, they should probably just be themselves? Carl Farber, a Dolan man who helped burn the Regulators out of the McSween house. Martin Teebs, the cowardly hero who tried in vain to protect McSween from being shot to bits during the escape (and failed miserably). Farber fixated on whether to address the question to Martin now, or wait for another meeting? While neither of them had shown up in any history books, they each could lay claim to being a Lincoln County warrior. Of course, reasoned Carl, if they were going to lean on their history, then they would have to be ok with *any* of it being brought to light. Based on his final night in Lincoln, he knew that could never, ever happen. With the moment slipping away, Farber decided that he needed more time to figure out how to approach this sensitive issue, and tabled his mental discussion for another day. "Hey, I'll see you at the next meeting ok? I mean, we don't have 'that' anymore, but at least we can have this, huh buddy?" Farber swept his good arm across the front of the barren strip mall to emphasize what he meant by "this".

Buddy? Is that what he was to Farber now? Just two weeks before they'd tried to kill each other, and now they were talking like old friends. Martin gave in and said, "Sure, see you then Carl." with a smile. Both men got in their cars and quietly drove away, Martin lost in his thoughts of the past and Farber lost in his of the future.

74

On a bright Saturday morning a few weeks later, Martin raced around the house, making preparations for the afternoon's cookout. Lilly held down the kitchen while he moved chairs, tables, grills, and coolers so as to make the Teebs' home look like they had these types of parties every weekend. "Martin!" cried Lilly from the kitchen, "Are you going to put the steaks on? They'll be here soon!"

Martin glided back into the kitchen. "Never fear my dear, because Martin Teebs is here. The steaks are all ready to hit that grill as soon as that doorbell rings."

"Well good, chef of the future, because the meat is all on you." his wife replied. Martin considered some kind of that's-what-she-said joke but decided that if it didn't go over, it could tamp down the current festive mood. Lilly looked around the kitchen happily. Martin had been back to his usual cheery self for the past few weeks. Because of his little pretend-to-be-an-outlaw gang she'd met a new friend, Jane, whom Lilly enjoyed getting to know. Martin had even made a new friend, a history teacher from town who shared his same silly passion for the old west and all things Billy the Kid. Life was seemingly back to almost normal, or even better, and the prospects of it staying that way gave Lilly hope. With the clock sitting just before 1pm Lilly chopped vegetables for the salad as she spoke, "I can't wait for Carl and Jane to get here. She's awesome. I just love her, don't you?"

"Yeah, she's great. And she seems like she's good for Farber. I couldn't stand that guy when I met him. Took a long time for me to come around." replied Martin.

Lilly cocked her head, looking puzzled, "Long time? You told me that you guys just met at your little history thingy a few weeks ago, didn't you?" Martin froze like a deer in the headlights for a brief moment. Of course, Lilly knew nothing about his history with Farber. Of course she could never know that, for if she did, she would also know about…..

"Yeah, that's what I mean Lil," he finally offered, "that first time I didn't think we'd get along…that's all." Lilly seemed fine with his answer and resumed her chopping as the doorbell rang. Martin pranced down the hall while announcing "I'll get it" to no one in particular. Opening the door, he saw not Farber but his work buddy Colin.

"Marty! Good to see you man, thanks for the invite." said a very obviously happy Colin. "This is Desiree, my…" Colin paused as if to get permission to say the word, "my girlfriend, right Des?"

Desiree, if that was her real name, was dressed in bright pink hot pants, a bikini top with a form fitting tank top stretched over it, and 5 inch heels that would make a drag queen jealous. If she wasn't a stripper in real life, she could easily play one on TV. The mismatch of the tall, thin, dorky Colin and the exotic sexuality of his girlfriend was almost too much for Martin to take in.

Grinning, Martin offered his hand, saying "Hi Desiree, Colin has talked about you a lot at work. Wonderful to finally meet you." Desiree offered up her hand and pursed her Botox inflamed lips. She offered merely a "Thank you" in a heavy accent that Martin guessed to be from Kyiv, or maybe Moscow? As he showed them down the hall, Farber and Jane walked up to the stairs and Martin greeted them as if old friends. Farber craned his head and neck around, trying to get a clear look at Desiree's ass. He gave Martin a chummy wink and scooted around the big man to get a better view. Lilly, making her way down the hall, jumped into the greeting festivities and the entire party moved out into the backyard under a sparkling sunny sky.

75

Now settled in the backyard, the three women sat around the table, drinking fruity, festive drinks and getting to know each other better. "So Desiree, where did you meet Colin? You two are such a cute couple!" gushed Jane.

"Ah, we met at work." Desiree said seemingly remembering the moment they met with a distant smile.

"Oh, I didn't know you worked with Martin and Colin? You're in advertising?" interjected Lilly.

"No silly," Desiree laughed, waving off any thought of an office job, "we met at *my* work. I'm a dancer".

Jane cocked her head with interest and asked, "Ballet?"

Desiree, remembering the shower of dollar bills Colin rained upon her when they first met, smiled to herself and quietly answered, "Something like that, yes...."

Martin manned the grill, the thick cut steaks dropping their juices onto the piping hot charcoal below. With each drop, a tiny burst of steam shot up and stung Martin's eyes. Farber slipped up behind him and put his hand on Martin's shoulder, "Where'd you get the steaks? Kellers?"

"Yeah," Martin replied, "They're the best I could find, but it's nothing like a freshly butchered yearling". Martin's misting eyes didn't escape the attention of Farber, who knew the waterworks weren't the byproduct of the grill. He clapped Martin on the back and said, "Hey, buddy. We've got it good here. Beautiful women, cold beer, steaks on the grill, and look, no one is shooting at us!"

Martin had to agree that not being marked for death was probably a good thing, but the reenacting group hadn't done a thing to satisfy his need for Lincoln, if anything, it had stoked it.

"We can't go back there Martin," Farber continued, "*remember*, we said that? You do remember, right?" Farber's firm inquest might have seemed to be spoken to protect Martin from being hurt further, but it really served to assure that his past secrets were kept in the past…where Farber firmly believed they belonged.

Colin walked over to join the men. "Hey Carl, you're a member of that Billy the Kid acting group too huh?" asked Colin naively.

"Reenacting group that is," corrected Farber, "and yes, I actually started it."

Colin, with no interest in the past, even his own, didn't have much more to offer to the conversation he started so Farber jumped in again, "Colin, maybe you should join us? We need a John Tunstall. Hell, you'd only have to be there for one meeting before you get killed!" Farber roared in laughter at the joke while Colin looked at Martin to see if it was even funny. Martin just shook his head and rolled his eyes at Farber.

"History's not my thing, women are." Colin said motioning towards Desiree who seemed to be showing the other ladies how to twerk. Farber's eyes opened wide, wondering if Jane was going to add this new move to her repertoire later in the day, and hoping she would. "Well, with that, I'm going to get another beer." announced Colin and drifted back towards the women.

Farber turned his attention back to his friend, who seemed to be struggling to maintain his interest in the present, and his composure, "It'll be ok Martin. This is where we belong amigo. Focus on the here and now." Farber said as Martin looked longingly through the smoke into a past only he could see.

"Well, here and now it's almost time to eat. Keep an eye on the steaks, will you? I need to grab the salad." said Martin as he slowly started shuffling into the house.

Farber fished into his pocket and withdrew a small fold of bills. Extracting a one-dollar bill and waving it in Martin's face he said, "Sure will pard, and, I might even see if I can get myself a lap dance from Colin's date!" Martin again rolled his eyes and shook his head as he walked into the kitchen. As the party continued and music drifted into the kitchen, Martin was surprised to hear the doorbell ring again. He and Lilly hadn't invited anyone else, and rarely would anyone deliver anything on Saturday. Even if they did, Martin had long since stopped ordering books about Billy the Kid, as no book could replace the real-life experiences Martin had with the young man.

He ambled down the hallway and swung open the front door. As he did, Martin's jaw hit the floor.

"What the fuck are you doing here?" he asked slowly of none other than his pal William H. Bonney, live and in the flesh.

"Teebsie! How ya been you big galloot?" chirped Billy in his familiar voice.

Martin's brain was short circuiting. How was the real Billy the Kid standing at his front door in the year 2020? He stammered out the question, "How did you, I mean where did you….?"

Billy jumped in to save his friend before Martin's head exploded, "You remember this don't cha?" Billy held out Bachaca's book, the same one that Martin had lost in what seemed a lifetime ago. Breathing heavily Martin answered simply, "Yeah."

"Well Teebsie, you left this in here. Prolly a bookmark I guess?" said Billy handing a yellowed receipt from the Waldwick Dry Cleanery to Martin. "Now, there weren't no Waldwick, New Jersey in 1878, but I made my way east and figured I'd just find it when I got to whatever the hell year this is," said Billy matter of factly, then continuing, "and here the hell I am!" Martin's head was spinning. Never in a million years did he think he'd ever see Billy again, and never in a billion years did he imagine it would be on his front steps in 2020.

"Listen Billy," Martin hissed quickly and quietly, "thank you for coming here, but I'm not going back to Lincoln, not ever. I can't. That part of my life is over. I has to be." Billy smirked at Martin the way he usually did, as if listening to someone who had no idea what they were even talking about. "You need to leave, however you got here. No one can see you here, you understand?" Martin was almost shouting now at the thought of Lilly seeing a long dead outlaw and inviting him in for a steak and a beer.

"Calm those oversize drawers Teebsie, I ain't here for you. I'm here cause of your boy." said Billy, just as something over Martin's shoulder caught his eye.

Carl Farber had abandoned his post at the grill and came walking down the hallway, in search of a bathroom. Like a bullet from a gun Billy saw him and screamed, "Cocksucker! I'll kill you!!" as he bolted past an astonished Martin and down the hall. Farber looked as if he'd seen a ghost and turned to run, just before the young man caught up with him. They rounded the corner and crashed into the guestroom with a mighty thud, both men hitting the floor to the sound of breaking glass announcing their entrance.

76

Martin sprinted around the corner, arriving at the guestroom just in time to see Billy pummeling the older and much bigger man into oblivion. Raining blows down from above, Billy was screaming a string of curses as Farber did his best to cover up. "Billy!" shouted Martin, attempting to pull the young man off of Farber, "What they hell are you doing?" Martin was able to grab his collar and drag Billy far enough away so that Farber could scoot backwards against the wall like a crab. He eyes glared both fear and anger at the young outlaw, "Crazy bastard! What the hell is your problem?" he screamed as a trickle of blood ran down his cheek.

Martin held Billy's collar, afraid of another attack if he let go. "Is this about his book? The one he wrote about you?" Martin asked urgently.

Billy growled, "This ain't about no book," then pointing menacingly at Farber, "this piece of shit…." Whatever Billy was going to say would have to wait, as Lilly Teebs made her presence known at the guestroom door. The crashing, cussing, and fighting was clearly audible to the ladies in the backyard, so Lilly quickly excused herself to find out what was going on.

"What's this? What is going on here? Martin?" she asked accusingly, figuring that since it was their house, her husband should answer for the spectacle she was seeing in front of her.

Martin felt the fight go out of Billy upon the arrival of a woman, so he released his collar. Getting no answer as the men glared at each others Lilly spoke more urgently, "Who are you, young man?" staring straight into Billy's blue eyes so it was clear who she was talking to.

Ever the gentleman Billy doffed his hat as he replied "How do Ma'am. I'm William H. Bonney. People call me Billy though." Throughout Martin's silly fascination with Billy the Kid, she had seen his clothes, his replica guns, and the numerous books that crowded every flat surface in their living room. She had even seen his ridiculous reenacting group with their patchwork outfits and wooden dummy revolvers. Something told her this was different. She had never seen this person before and something about him seemed….real.

With her brain processing what she was seeing, she was only able to squeeze out an incredulous, "What?"

"I'm a friend of your husband Ma'am." said Billy through his crooked smile. Unsure of what was really happening, Lilly glared first at Farber, who avoided her eyes, and then at Martin who defiantly matched them.

"And I'm here," Billy continued, pointing menacingly at Farber, "because this piece of shit raped his girlfriend Rosita and I aim to kill him!"

Martin froze, his heart having stopped beating for a moment. Then, his blood ran cold, imagining the man he now considered a friend forcing himself on his woman, pregnant with Martin's child. Upon hearing the news, if it was actually true, Lilly swallowed hard and looked at Martin to see if his eyes betrayed anything. She'd have to wait though, until Martin's murderous gaze settled on the simpering Farber who realized that the genie was out of the lamp, and he could hide from his hideous past no more.

Trying to deflect the attention, and perhaps a bullet, Farber blurted out quickly towards Lilly, while pointing at her husband, "He's having a baby with Rosita!"

A roar, commonly heard from the biggest jungle cats escaped Lilly's throat at the news, "What????"

Seeing that he might just talk his way out of the situation, Farber decided to pile on, "Yeah, and he killed a man too. A deputy! Shot him right between the eyes! Hell," said Farber figuring he should fire all of his bullets at once, "he shot me too. How do you think I got this hole in my arm?" Martin was now sitting at the bottom of a very large pile of shit that had just been dumped on him. Just moments ago he was the savior, pulling Billy away from his buddy Farber over what was surely a misunderstanding. Now, in the space of moments, his life was unraveling before his eyes, and his ears. With nothing to lose, and knowing that Farber wouldn't be attending anymore Saturday barbeques, Martin pulled the last bullet from his arsenal and aimed it straight at Farber.

"He wrote a book about you," said Martin, talking to Billy but pointing to the still quivering Farber, "calling you the coward of Lincoln County!"

Billy's hair trigger snapped again screaming, "Coward my ass!!" as he lunged at Farber. Grabbing the older man by the collar, he hauled off to break his nose when the room was shocked into submission by a screaming Lilly Teebs.

"ENOUGH!!!" she roared above the din, in a voice loud enough to stop everyone in their tracks.

The 4-way Mexican standoff stood silently, eyeing each other, each wondering who would make the next move. Finally, his composure restored, Billy spoke, "Well then, since we's all telling secrets about each other, how's about you share one? You know, to break the tension and all." Billy allowed a cocky smile to permeate his lips, making Lilly wonder what the boy thought he knew about her?

Looking confused, overwhelmed by what she was seeing, and a bit nervous Lilly glanced from Martin to Billy to Farber. Just then Jane burst into the room. Her confusion and panic was obvious. Farber was bleeding from the mouth and maybe his head, Martin was drenched in sweat, and one of the reenactors who she'd never seen was balling his fists as if ready for another fight.

"Uh, Lilly. Your phone was ringing. It rang a couple of times. I thought maybe I should answer it. It's your doctor." said Jane as she slowly handed the phone to her new friend.

Lilly lifted the phone to her ear. "Yes, this is Lilly Teebs," she said blankly into the mouthpiece, "Uh huh. What?" said Lilly and then paused as if she didn't know what else to say. "Are you certain?" she asked in an emotionless monotone. Without disconnecting the call, her arm dropped to her side, and then the phone dropped from her fingers, crashing onto the floor. Her other arm went to her stomach, as if she might retch. When she spoke it was flat, as if something inside her had just died, "I'm pregnant." was all she said.

Lilly turned and walked zombie-like, out of the room. Martin, his mind racing to the use of condoms *every single time* they made love, tried to understand what was happening. He began to follow her when Billy spoke, "Teebsie, what about him?" as he gestured toward the bloody, battered, and scared Carl Farber.

Nearly catatonic after the events of the past few minutes, Martin slowly reached into his pocket and pulled out a small key ring. He sifted through the keys until he found the one he sought. He opened the nightstand door to reveal a small safe. Without a word Martin slipped the key in, opened the safe, and let the lid pop up to reveal his 1873 Colt single action Army revolver with a 4 ¾ inch barrel. The gun was loaded with 4 live rounds and the hammer rested on one of two empty shell casings. That was the bullet he had fired into Farber's arm. As Martin turned to walk out of the room a giant smile filled Billy's face as Farber screamed and cowered in the corner in horror. For his part, Martin Teebs never even looked back to see what happened next.

77

One Year Later:

Martin sat quietly on the sofa as he flicked the TV remote. The screen fizzed for just a moment before a picture popped up, almost against its will. The house was still as its only remaining inhabitant was about to settle in for some Sunday afternoon football. Eagles vs Giants was always a great rivalry, and Martin knew he could burn through 3 hours or more without having to focus on anything else. These days, an escape from his reality was more than just a luxury, it was a mental health necessity. Just as the opening kickoff sailed through the air, the doorbell rang. Martin, expecting no one, peaked through the peephole and slowly opened the door. On his front step was a kindly looking older gentleman. He wore a loose pair of blue jeans with a tan jacket, and a worn baseball cap. His face was covered with a beard, but Martin somehow felt they had met before. The familiarity nagged at him for a moment. Unable to remember who this person might be, he spoke, "Can I help you?"

The man, whose body language showed he did not want to be perceived as a threat or a door to door solicitor, stepped back a bit before speaking in a gentle, reassuring voice "Are you Martin Teebs?"

Now Martin eyed the man suspiciously, unable to shake the feeling they had already met, answered, "Yes I am. Who are you?"

Still smiling the man fidgeted, but finally spoke, "My name is Scot. Scot Scurlock." Pouring a bucket of ice water down Martin's back would have produced the same effect as hearing the last name of one of his old Lincoln County War pals.

"Scurlock, as in Doc Scurlock?" Martin asked, fervently hoping that the answer would be no.

"Yes Sir, he was my great grandpa." sighed Scot, somehow wishing he no longer had to go through with his mission. Martin had no idea how to proceed. In his right ear he heard voluminous cheering, and he suspected that the Giants had done something good for a change. He wanted this kindly man to simply disappear. He wanted him to turn and walk away and never return again. He wanted his doorbell to never have been rung, but Martin knew there had to be a reason for the visit, and his curiosity got the better of him.

"What can I do for you Scot?" he said formally.

"Um Martin, this is for you." said Scurlock, handing him the faded yellow envelope he'd been carrying in his back pocket.

Martin looked at the envelope, still sealed, and wondered what was inside. It appeared to be a 100 years old with deep creases in the many folds it had acquired over the years. In bold block print on the front it said:

TO BE OPENED ONLY BY MARTIN TEEBS OF WALDWICK, NJ
DELIVER BY SEPTEMBER 2021

Martin's eyes were transfixed on the writing as he asked, "Where did you get this?"

"From my auntie," answered Scot, "Before her I think from my grandpa, and before that…" Scot didn't finish as he didn't want to guess what the envelope's purpose was. The story of it had been loosely handed down among his family but he didn't want to irritate Martin with hearsay. "Anyway," he continued, "she made me promise to deliver it just before she passed. Said I needed to get it to you, or I would have to pass it on to someone in my family that would. And….here I am."
Now sure that the envelope contained something he definitely did not want to read, he asked simply, "What is it?"

Scot's eyes saddened a bit as he spoke, "I don't know Martin. No one's ever opened it. My auntie said that you'd know what to do with it." Martin glanced from the letter to Scot several times. He considered laughing and telling Scot he was only kidding and that he wasn't Martin Teebs, but in the end he knew his fate was somehow tied to whatever was inside the ancient envelope.

"Is there something I should know Martin?" asked Scot gently, "I mean, how could someone from so long ago know you were going to exist, much less know where you would live?"

Martin had no answer so decided to end the conversation. He patted Scot on the shoulder as he spoke "Thanks Scot. Really. Thanks" Scot Scurlock smiled and turned to walk away, his family's sworn duty finally fulfilled. Halfway down the brick walkway he turned and looked Martin straight in the eyes. "Good luck Martin." he said with a friendly wave of his hand. Martin stood watching him as he slowly walked to the corner, and then out of sight.

78

With the crowd roaring over a Carson Wentz screen pass that the Eagles had turned into the go-ahead touchdown, Martin sat carefully on the sofa and inspected the envelope again. The sounds of the game receded into the background as he plucked at it ,and coaxed the well-worn letter out. With the same deep creases as the envelope, Martin took his time opening it, not wanting to damage whatever message had come for him from his past. It said simply:

887 Kelly Road Magdalena, NM – Please come by September 17, 1940 IMPORTANT!

Staring at the neat printing for what seemed like hours, Martin finally shuddered and placed the letter back in the envelope.

79

Magdalena, NM September 17, 1940

A frail, elderly man sat wrapped in a blanket on the rocking chair on his front porch. He and his wife Maria had built and lived in this small house on the outskirts of Magdalena for almost 60 years. The man was in poor health, coughing fitfully. In his prime, the man was known as William H. Bonney, but now most people just called him Billy Antrim, and on this day he was celebrating his 81st birthday.

Doc Scurlock, now almost 90 but in far better health than Billy, exited the house in his undershirt, pants, and a pair of suspenders. Carrying a pipe and wearing a wide brimmed fedora the older man was in good spirits. Strong and wiry in his old age, Doc had come from Texas to celebrate his friend's birthday as he'd done every year since the turn of the century.

"Hey Kid, Happy Birthday!" beamed Doc.

Billy looked morose. He'd never enjoyed a birthday after he turned 21. Every one of them seemed to mark some secret torment that the man carried around with him, and as such, birthdays were no reason to celebrate.

"This shoulda been over a long time ago Doc." whispered Billy, his lungs full of fluid, making it difficult to talk or breath.

Doc smiled sadly at his longtime friend, knowing exactly what he meant. If Doc could say something to cheer him up, he would have, but previous birthdays told him that Billy was more interested in waiting to die than wanting to live. With nothing left to say between the two men, a delivery truck drove up and a large, brawny man who appeared to be in his 60's stepped out.

"Junior, you made it!" croaked Billy as loudly as he could. The big man bent over and gave Billy a giant warm hug, genuinely happy to see him.

"Hey Junior, good to see you kid. How ya been?" asked Doc warmly while in the midst of a strong handshake with the man.

"Been good Doc, you?" asked Junior. Seeing Doc nod to the affirmative, Junior continued "I don't leave Lincoln much no more."

Before the uneasiness that surely would follow could creep into their conversation, the door opened and two children spilled out to greet their grandpa. "Papa!" the kids shouted, "you came for Bisobuelo's birthday party. Yay!!"

Junior bent over and scooped up one grandchild in each arm, his eyes alight at seeing his own flesh and blood, "Tomas, Ronita! My babies!" Junior twirled the kids in a circle until they laughed themselves into a tizzy. He carefully placed them down and they scooted off the porch to play in the desert.

"Will you stay the night, Junior?" asked Billy hopefully, "We've got room."

"I can't Pops. I need to get back to Lincoln in case…." Junior didn't finish his thought, knowing where the conversation would lead. "I just need to get back to Lincoln." he said simply. Billy and Doc looked sadly at each other as Junior looked off into the distance. They knew the pain he'd been in all of his life. Billy secretly wished that somehow, Martin would find a fold in time that would allow him to meet his only son, just once…but that meeting had never happened and Junior had spent his life…waiting.

"He'da come back by now if he could Junior. You know that." offered Doc in an attempt to smooth over Junior's bubbling anger. Regrettably his tactic failed, launching Junior into the tirade they all hoped to avoid.

"I don't know anything of the sort Doc! I don't even know my father because he left before I was born and was too much of a God damned coward to ever come back!" yelled Junior, his volume and anger rising at each word. Unable to take any more Billy collected himself. "Easy Junior!" he snapped, "That's my friend you're talking about. Don't you forget that". The effort pushed Billy into a coughing fit as his lungs bubbled and fizzed. Both Doc and Junior rushed to his side, trying to calm him, but Billy waved them off to continue the struggle on his own. Junior hung his head, having upset the only man who was ever really a father to him. He hated himself for what he'd just done in that moment, only slightly less than he hated the memory of Martin Teebs.

"Shit, I'm sorry Pops," he said genuinely, "I didn't want to cause a fuss on your birthday" Billy nodded and weakly waved his hand to tell Junior it was ok.

"A man waits 60 years for his father to show up, it wears on you," continued Junior sadly, then adding a quiet and sad, "60 years….." for no one's benefit but his own.

"Your father was a good man. Decent man," said Doc, still trying to placate Junior, "did the best he could under the circumstances."

"Well, you couldn't prove that by me Doc" said Junior sternly, "where was your friend when my mama needed him most? Huh?" Junior's eyes dared either man to come up with a satisfactory explanation, but they could not. Junior's face blazed with anger, not at Billy or Doc, but at the memory of a man who abandoned his family and left them all to suffer his absence. With Billy sitting sadly in his chair, Junior folded his arms and looked out to the vast desert surrounding the lonely house. Doc, upset at seeing his friends argue, retreated into the house. He rifled through the tiny desk that Maria used to write out her Christmas cards and letters to family in Mexico. Finding a sheet of paper and an envelope, he sat down and carefully wrote out the envelope in big block letters:

TO BE OPENED ONLY BY MARTIN TEEBS OF WALDWICK, NJ
DELIVER BY SEPTEMBER 2021

80

Doc rejoined the men on the porch, still not speaking to each other. He went over and gave Billy a rub on his now bald scalp and patted Junior on the shoulder. Everyone seemed sad at the turn their conversation had taken. The quiet between them threatened to stretch to an eternity. "I'm going Pops. I've done enough damage on your birthday. I love you." said Junior as he leaned over to kiss Billy on top of the head. Billy's eyes teared up but he couldn't find any words to comfort Junior or himself, or to convince him to stay. Junior slowly climbed into the truck and drove away, the truck trailing dust behind it as it went.

Billy looked around, his lips quivering, lost. Burdened by the fact that he cheated the grim reaper out of 60 more years than he was due, he let his tears fall noiselessly from his eyes before he spoke. "I want to go Doc. I don't wanna be here no more." he said in a small and sad voice. If he'd had the strength, he'd have retrieved his Colt and done the deed to himself right there on the porch. Then, the thought of Maria rushing out to see what he'd done came to mind. He saw Tomas and Ronita running to see what was wrong as Maria screamed to keep them away. He saw Doc having to scoop up what was left of his brains before anyone else saw them. He saw complete devastation to those he loved. He was trapped, trapped in a life he wanted no part of anymore.

"C'mon Billy. It's your birthday. We can be happy about that, no?" said Doc trying to cheer the old outlaw out of his funk.

"No!" screamed Billy, "I had too many damned birthdays. 60 more than I was supposed to get! I should be under the dirt in Sumner with Charlie and Tom. It outta be *ME* there! Not….." Billy pressed his eyes tightly together, remembering a night so long ago, but that still seemed like yesterday. A small choking sound came from his lips at the thought.

Doc carefully tried to talk his friend down, knowing the shouting was no good for his congested lungs, "Billy…." he said calmly.

"Billy nuthin!" railed the old man "Teebsie was right. I had no business having this damned book!"

PAGE 241

Billy produced the well worn and aged copy of Sergio Bachaca's book that Martin had lost during Brady's murder all those years ago from under his blanket. The book that wouldn't be written for another 60 years or so. The book that detailed every event of his life right up until the time that Pat Garrett was supposed to have gunned him down near midnight in Fort Sumner on July 14, 1881. That book. That book that allowed him to escape his fate while sealing another's. Billy hated the book, and he hated himself for reading it. Surely he would have known when Charlie Bowdre, Tom Folliard, Alexander McSween, and others would die. Surely he could have saved them all. But just as surely, he didn't. Billy took a front row seat to history and watched his friends being slaughtered when he could have stopped every bit of it. The sad part of it all was, he didn't even know why? That thought tormented him on every single September 17th thereafter. Each birthday a reminder that his friends were dead, he was not, and he deserved to be with them.

Billy weakly threw the book on the porch while saying, "I wish to hell I would have given it back to him," and then more softly, "I wish to hell I was dead and buried where I belong Doc."

If Doc heard Billy's final wish, he didn't betray it, his eyes transfixed as a dusty pickup truck rolled to a stop in front of the porch. Whoever was in the back jumped out and thanked the driver as the truck pulled away. As the dust cleared Doc couldn't restrain himself, "Son of a bitch…." Martin Teebs squinted and walked slowly toward the porch, unsure of who he was here to see and why he was here to see them. As he reached the steps, he sighted a sickly old man whose familiar blue eyes still pierced him when they connected.

"Billy? Billy, is that you?" asked Martin incredulously

Billy's eyes opened wide, but he could find no words. Martin looked to his left and saw a man who was nearly the spitting image of the Scot Scurlock, who had been on his porch just a few days earlier. "Jesus Christ, Doc? Is that you?" asked the amazed time traveler.

Doc smiled warmly, extending his hand and saying, "You got my letter, huh Martin?"

Martin reached into his back pocket to produce the worn letter that Doc had written only minutes ago. Doc smiled outwardly but sighed heavily on the inside knowing the letter didn't serve its intended purpose. Billy's lip began to quiver, bracing himself to greet his old friend. "Oh shit, I think I musta died and gone to hell," laughed Billy through his pain, "Teebsie my friend, what are you doing here?"

"Doc sent me a message." replied Martin.

Billy looked thankfully at Doc and began to cry again. "I'm sorry bout this Teebsie. Bout all of it." he said through his tears.

Sensing that Billy was very ill, and not wanting to upset his friend, Martin gently replied, "Billy, don't. It's ok."

"Ok nothing! I been waiting 60 years to say this. I was wrong. I had no business keeping that damned book. No man should know his future so he don't try to change it." said Billy as he descended into a severe coughing fit.

"That doesn't matter now Billy." said Martin, hoping he could calm his friend.

Billy stopped coughing but had no more energy to yell. "It matters to me Teebsie. I didn't do no good cept for myself with that thing. You'll find out. I just set and watched everyone else die. It's a terrible thing, knowing your own fate. It ain't no gift. It's a curse." he said between his shallow, struggling breaths.

Billy began to sob loudly as Martin pulled up a stool next to him. He cradled the withering old man in his arms as he began to cry too. Billy's breathing began to slow, and his face twitched. From deep inside, Martin heard the bubbling in the old man's lungs. His breathing slowed further, as if he'd given up on trying to remain alive anymore. Slowly rocking him, Martin could feel the life slipping away from the boy bandit. Billy opened his eyes and croaked, "I love you Teebsie. Always did. I'm so sorry my friend."

Martin's tears poured from his eyes like New Mexico's summer monsoon rains, staining the blanket that held the best friend he'd ever had in life, as he whispered into Billy's ear, "I love you too Billy".

Billy coughed sharply, his body going rigid. His eyes continued to drain as Martin felt the last bit of life drift from his friend. Going limp, Billy's sharp blue eyes glassed over and the light behind them simply went out. Billy the Kid, was dead. What Pat Garrett had failed to do, Father Time finally achieved.

"He's gone?" asked Martin of Doc, unsure of what to do.

"Yeah. He's gone," said Doc with a nod of his head, "Good life though. He had a good life Martin." Doc walked over and rubbed his hand on Billy's still warm head. He gently reached down and closed his eyes as Martin still rocked his friend slightly back and forth.

"I'm sorry too Martin" said Doc contemplatively as he lit his pipe.

"For what Doc?" Martin asked

"For my message. It got there too late." said Doc, his eyes averted from what he knew he must tell Martin. Martin looked confused. He looked at his friend Billy's body lifeless in his arms. He assumed he'd been summoned here to say goodbye. He didn't yet understand Doc's message was meant to have him say hello.

"Your boy was just here," said Doc as he stared over the vast, dusty plain, "Left just before you arrived. Been waiting 60 years to meet his Daddy." Doc looked down at the wooden porch and shook his head sadly. "If I'da been a little quicker you'da finally met him. Things woulda been different. Damn ,would things have been different."

Martin's lip quivered and his eyes stung with the tears of a man who had lost everything…again. All he could manage by way of response was to choke out a simple, "What?" Doc inhaled deeply from his pipe and just shook his head.
Martin's head rolled back against the wall as his tears ran unabated to the ground. His son, his one and only, had been there, and Martin missed him. He sobbed loudly and uncontrollably as he hung his head in sorrow.

"I hope to hell you find a way to meet that boy just once before he's gone Martin. That would be some sight. I wish I could be there to see what you'd say to each other," said Doc "I'm sure it'd be something beautiful." Martin buried his head in his hands as 140 years of love, loss, death, friendship, and hardship poured out of him. His two crazy lives flashed before his mind's eye. He was alone, with no one, and with nothing. He'd lost everything he'd ever known or loved and missed out on loving the one thing he wanted more than anything in the world. The only flesh and blood that he had left on the planet had gone, and Martin knew he could not follow. The letter brought him here. He had no way to get there.

If Martin Teebs had decided to curl up and die next to his famous outlaw friend, no one would have blamed him. As it was, there wasn't even anyone left to care enough to stop him. Martin sobbed heavily, his body shuddering with each breath, as his now dead friend Billy departed this world, hopefully bound for a better life in the next. Doc dragged deeply on his pipe and exhaled, the smoke curling off the porch and rising upwards towards the sky. It swirled in the air, joining the clouds in a circle that would remain unbroken and eternal…

Just like time.

The End.

ABOUT THE AUTHOR

Michael Anthony Giudicissi is an author, screenwriter, and speaker from Albuquerque, NM. Michael hosts the internationally popular YouTube channel, "All Things Billy the Kid". In addition to the Back to Billy series, Michael has written a number of other books focused on personal growth, business, and sales.

Disclaimer: *Due to the shifting nature of fiction versus reality, we're unsure exactly who is currently writing these books.* Clearly a fictional character named Martin Teebs is not writing them, but who is Martin Teebs, really? Recent reports point to the fact that a Martin Teebs might just exist after all. We're not clear on whether Michael Anthony Giudicissi is a real person, or perhaps Michael Roberts might be the driving force behind the manuscript. It's possible, as disagreeable as it may seem, that even Carl Farber could be at the helm of current and future Back to Billy stories. Anyone with any information on this vexing puzzle is encouraged to contact the "author" at the links below.

To Contact the Author: billythekidridesagain@gmail.com

Books in the "Back to Billy" saga:
Back to Billy – 2nd Edition (Mankind Media, 2023)
1877 (Mankind Media 2021)
Sunset in Sumner (Mankind Media 2021)
Bonney and Teebs (Mankind Media 2021)
One Week in Lincoln (Mankind Media 2021)
4 Empty Graves (Mankind Media 2022)

COMING SOON:
Pieces of Us, Book 7 in the Back to Billy Saga (Mankind Media 2023)
1950, Book 8 in the Back to Billy Saga (Mankind Media 2023)